DON'T EAT
THE RED CORN

DON'T EAT THE RED CORN

PRAKASH SESHADRI

Prakash Seshadri Wilmington 2016

ISBN: 0996319328
ISBN 13: 9780996319324
Library of Congress Control Number: 2016920593
LCCN imprint: Prakash Seshadri: Wilmington, Delaware

This book is a work of fiction. Names, characters, businesses, places, events and incidents are either the products of the author's imagination or used in a fictitious manner. Any resemblance to actual persons, living or dead, or actual events is purely coincidental.

To my family for all their encouragement.

TABLE OF CONTENTS

Chapter 1

The light of the midday sun reflected off the orange clay tile covering a majestic Spanish Revival home with cream stucco. The three-story home had two upper floors with Juliet and standard balconies adorned with wrought-iron railings in an intricate, glossy-black design of swirls mixed with ears of corn. This design was copied from a home in the New Orleans Garden District. None of the detail could be seen from the two-lane highway in front of the house, as the dwelling was hidden behind large, lush line of arborvitae and a stucco fence that matched the homes walls. Roses were scattered around the property and competed with honeysuckle creeping on the sides of the house for best fragrance.

The dark sedan drove past the open wrought-iron gates and rumbled slowly on the brick driveway, stopping near a beautiful cement fountain. The fountain had cherubs flying in an imaginary heaven where they were playing water games with water flowing from one jug to another in a frozen scene.

The door of the dark-blue sedan opened. A man about five foot six stepped out. His matte-black shoes exited the vehicle first. His hair was wavy and coated in hair gel so that the slight breeze of the day barely moved the waves. He had a pudgy nose and a stubbly beard. His eyes had crow's-feet that identified him as being at least in his upper forties. The corners of his mouth pointed downward as if there was something to scowl at. His mouth looked as if it desired something to hang from it, possibly a toothpick or cigarette. He wore a dark-blue satin jacket with police insignia on the arms. The jacket looked heavier than the weather called for, as it was a beautiful, warm late summer day.

Sammy Grillo closed the door on the Crown Victoria and looked around at the impressive property in front of him, noting two other police vehicles with their flashing lights on in the more obvious colors of black and white. Sammy noticed how out of place the cars were in front of what looked like an ancient abode that had had additions built on over the years. The structure was the same age as other developments in the area but was distinct, as it did not have a cookie-cutter floor plan. In front of the home's dark, sturdy wooden entryway was a tall, capped officer talking with a heavyset, curly haired woman. Sammy approached the officer. Behind Sammy, the driver of the Crown Victoria, a thin, young man, followed behind him close enough to step on his shadow. The tall officer turned from the weeping woman and approached Sammy.

"What do you have, Joe?" Sammy asked the tall officer in his Brooklyn accent.

"Well, I'm not sure, boss. It looks like a poisoning maybe. Looks bad. I haven't seen anything like this before. The mother, father, boy—all dead and bleeding. Looks awful," Joe Holden said very quickly and with some agitation. The fear seemed misplaced in the imposing, well-built figure, who wouldn't appear to be afraid of anything.

Sammy looked into Joe's long face and his wide nose and held up both his hands as if he were doing push-ups. "Joe, take it slowly and calmly from the beginning. First, who are you talking to?"

"Uh, she is Margarita Sanchez, the housekeeper. She came to do her morning cleaning and found the family. She's the one who called us to the scene." The pace of Joe's speech slowed as he began to relax.

The woman he was interviewing was about five feet tall and wore a skirted, light-gray uniform adorned with a white collar.

Sammy stood on his tiptoes and looked over Joe's left shoulder at the woman, who was visibly weeping with a handkerchief covering her nose. "And she has worked for them for a while?"

"Yes, she says about five years. She has had a very good relationship with the family. She said they thought of her as part of the family. She was very surprised to find them."

"Have you been inside?"

"Yes. The scene is surreal."

"OOOK," Sammy said mockingly. "You're not telling me anything by saying that. *Surreal* means nothing to me. I know that you guys are not used to looking at crime scenes, but you need to be more descriptive. Who else is with you?" Sammy doubted his colleague's descriptions, as he believed his officers were used to Mayberry-type crimes.

"George Westie. He's scoping out the place."

"I hope he's wearing gloves and booties," Sammy said sternly.

"Uh, no. We thought that somebody was still around so…" Joe said cautiously, knowing he and George had done something wrong.

"Well, was there?" Sammy raised his voice. He was thinking in the back of his mind that there was not.

"Uh, no," Joe said, again fearful.

"Get on your radio, and tell George to get out of there. Tell him to make sure he doesn't touch anything on his way out!" Sammy said, raising his voice even further.

Joe radioed George through his shoulder mic, telling him exactly what Sammy said.

Sammy turned his head toward the young officer who had driven him to the scene. The officer was staring off into space. "Lenny, wake up! Go into the trunk of the car, and get the box of booties and gloves."

The young man snapped to attention and ran toward their unmarked police vehicle. He opened the trunk and grabbed two rectangular boxes. He ran back and held the two boxes in front of Sammy's face.

Sammy took two booties and two gloves and put them on. "Lenny, put these on, and give a set to Joe."

"Yes, sir." Lenny obliged and put his gear on and then handed the coverings to Joe.

"I'm going to talk to Miss Sanchez here, and then we will go inside," Sammy said and approached the cleaning lady. But before he reached her, the door opened quickly as George came out.

"George, nice of you to join us. Lenny, hand George some gloves and booties," Sammy said, looking right at George.

George was a heavyset man, and his belt barely contained his belly. His sandy-colored hair was messy and partly covered his eyes. George hopped around to get his booties on.

"Sorry about that, Chief," George said. George was sincere, but he'd been upset that the town hired an outsider for the position of chief, when he was next in line.

Sammy turned to the weeping woman. "Sorry about this horrible crime, ma'am," Sammy said. He felt awkward. He was not accustomed to death, even though he was more familiar with homicide crime scenes than the rest of his department and had shied away from even family funerals. "I wanted to ask you just a few questions more about the family, if I may."

"If you need to," Miss Sanchez said, nearly choking on her tears.

"How were Mr. Mend and the Mend family yesterday? Were they acting normally?"

"Oh yes. Even better than usual during the week. Mr. Mend was usually so contemplative and quiet. But yesterday he was dancing a jig. It was incredible. It was like Christmas, and everyone—his wife, daughter, and son—was smiling and dancing for joy. They were so happy for their father. I think some new business was coming to him."

"Hmm. Did anyone have it out for him that you know of?" Sammy was beginning to think that after such a positive week for the family, at least per the housekeeper's account, murder/suicide was unlikely. Although he did believe it was still one of the possibilities.

"He spoke about a man with a generic-sounding name to his wife."

"Generic name. Hmm." Sammy raised his eyebrows at her, looking for more.

"Yes, yes, yes. It was, I believe, a Roger…Ingersoll. He was some board member or something," Miss Sanchez said but still sounded uncertain.

"So he wanted to harm the family?" Sammy tried to delve deeper, but he knew he was going to the extreme.

"Oh no, no, no. Mr. Mend made it sound as if it was completely business. Potentially, he could lose his business because of him. I am not sure. He never told me this. He would talk to his wife or on the phone, and I would hear. I wasn't eavesdropping, but if you are sweeping stairs or cleaning a toilet and someone is airing their dirty laundry on the phone or with one's spouse, you hear things."

"I understand. Did you prepare the family's food?" Sammy tried to make a connection with the housekeeper and the dead family within the house.

"Oh no, sir. Mrs. Mend was the cook of the house. She fancied herself a chef and would make all the family's food. She made some kind of stuffed cornbread the night before, and they had ears of corn as well. I had no taste for her offerings. I was honestly not a big fan of her cooking, and I would most days bring my lunch."

"So when did you leave yesterday?"

"I left last night right after dinner. The whole family was in a good mood because Mr. Mend was in a good mood."

"And so you found them here, dead, this morning?"

"Yes." Miss Sanchez clutched a handkerchief to her face and began to weep.

"OK, Miss Sanchez." Sammy put his hand on her shoulder. "Thank you. I think it would be best if you leave now, so that we can conduct the rest of our investigation. Joe, here, will get your contact information. Would it be OK to contact you if we need further information?"

"That would be fine. And please find out who did this to this very good family," she said, dabbing her eyes with a handkerchief as she moved toward Joe to give him her number.

Sammy looked at the polished wood door with its large black-painted iron hinges that ended in points. He squinted a little in fear of what he might find inside. "Lenny, George, come with me. Joe, check out back, and please don't lay your hands on anything without gloves."

Sammy, Lenny, and George walked into the house.

"So, George, you bumbled in here yourself. What have you found so far? Let's start on the lower level and work our way up." Sammy turned the iron doorknob with his fluorescent-blue gloved hand.

"Uh, I ran upstairs, thinking maybe someone was still alive," George said.

"And let's turn in here. Keep talking," Sammy said and opened a large, highly polished wooden door. He told George to talk, but he stopped listening after all three went into the office.

The door opened into a very neat and tidy room with a large, ornate wooden desk. Many carvings were on the legs, including lions' heads, and at the base of the legs were clawed feet. The walls were painted in a subtle green shade. Among numerous framed posters and articles on the wall was one from the *New Mexico Gazette* from the 1960s with the title, "Native New Mexican Makes a Run at the Big Seed Companies." The page was brown at the edges, and the text was fading, but a good-looking man not much older than his midtwenties in a dark suit, complete with skinny tie and white shirt, was still very visible. The man was sitting on a rock outside a farm. In addition, a few trade advertisements were on the walls. One was made of tin and had a large ear of corn painted diagonally on it with the company colors of red and yellow in the background. In smaller font it said, "If you want Quality yields and Quality taste, you need a Quality Seed."

Sammy heard a pen drop and turned quickly from the pictures. A small antique writing desk's top was open, and Lenny had knocked over one of the pencil holders. Annoyed that Lenny would be ruining his crime scene, Sammy told him to look only at the kitchen and living room. He turned his attention to George. "And what did you find?"

"The bodies are up there, on the second floor. The father was in the hall with a spilled glass of what looked like water in his hand. He was face down."

Sammy shut George off in his head again and approached the desk. He saw a bound sales report with a clear covering. The cover was white with a blue rectangle that held, in a giant font, a large white Q and in smaller font, the words, "The Q stands for Quality." The text in the smallest font on the page said, "Sales Report." Sammy carefully peeled back the cover of the report, leaving it on the desk. The report was dated yesterday. He cursorily looked at some of the charts and tables, which highlighted in a simple bar graph future sales rising to the highest sales in company history. He turned a few more pages and saw graphs with curves of competitors' market shares trending downward. Sammy had figured out why Mr. Mend was so happy last night.

"And the rest of the family?" Sammy asked George.

"As I was saying, sir, the mother was cuddling the son in the son's bed, frozen in place, and the son was lying still with no covers on him." George straightened out his belt.

"Did you move them or touch them?"

"I touched them, but they were cold. I felt for a pulse and listened for breathing. But I didn't move them at all."

"Well, let's hope so. We'll quickly peruse the rest of the first floor, see what Lenny found, and go upstairs."

Sammy and George walked out of the office into the foyer and then explored a formal living room.

"George, I hope you have your pocket camera. Take some pictures of the room."

George reached into his pocket and, after jiggling some keys, pulled a small camera out of his pocket. He started snapping pictures.

"We shoulda taken some pictures in the office. When we are done upstairs, take pictures of the walls, office, and some of that sales brochure."

"OK, boss."

Sammy walked from the living room into a formal dining room. From there he peered into the kitchen. He saw Lenny looking in the cabinets, reaching in and moving things around.

"Did you find anything?" Sammy asked.

Lenny closed the cabinet door he was looking in and stood straight up. He looked worried, like a kid who got caught with his hand in a cookie jar. A big wad of something was in his cheek. "No, sir," he said, trembling.

Sammy looked at a bowl by the sink, half-filled with corn muffins. A piece of a corn muffin on top of the mound was missing. He wondered what subject Lenny must have failed in the police academy—criminology or listening to your commanding officer.

"You know I told you not to touch anything—just look." Sammy stared right at him.

"Sorry, I just wanted to be thorough."

"Well, Lenny, I hope you didn't disturb any valuable evidence. You didn't happen to eat any of those muffins?"

"Oh, oh no." Lenny stammered his answer.

Sammy grew angrier, since he knew Lenny was lying to him. He didn't have anything against this new addition to the force, but in Sammy's career the police were to use greater vigilance against those who lied when asking a question. "Lenny, get out of here. Go see what Joe is doing in the yard, and again don't ruin any evidence. And Lenny, I hope you didn't eat any of that cornbread in that bowl, as it looks as if we may be dealing with a poisoning."

He was not sure how harsh he should be with Lenny. Lenny was a new officer right out of the academy, and if he was in New York, he would have learned via the school of hard knocks, as Sammy had. The young officer was the Barney Fife of the department, incompetent but harmless. He would have given him a harder time, but Lenny was the former chief's nephew, and the retired chief still had sway over the town council, who made decisions on Sammy's job security. He finished looking over the kitchen and barked out to George, "I think we have seen all we will see down here. Let's go upstairs where the action is."

George and Sammy walked into the foyer and then started up a beautiful spiral staircase. An ornate gold chandelier hung from the ceiling with many crystals bending light this way and that. Sammy started to smell the bodies.

"George, make sure you take pictures of how the bodies are positioned and their faces as well as any signs of trauma. Again, don't touch anything."

"OK, sir," George said and repositioned his belt after the stair climb.

The bodies lay in the same positions George had indicated. Sammy came across the patriarch lying in the hallway. To him, it looked as if the man was on his way to retrieve something and then was felled instantly with no rhyme or reason.

"The man does not look to have suffered or struggled with an assailant," Sammy said as he crouched down to inspect the man's face. He noticed dried blood coming from his nose. He studied the face for a moment.

"What do ya see?" George asked.

"Well, at the outset, I'm not sure this is a crime scene. But we should treat it as such until proven otherwise," Sammy told him.

"Well, the wife and son are over here when you are done looking at him." George motioned to an open door close to the body of Mr. Mend.

"That's the son's room, right?" Sammy asked.

"Yes, sir."

"Well, lemme check out the master first, and then I'll go in there," Sammy said. He stood up from Mr. Mend's body and walked to the furthest room down the hall.

The room was possibly 600square feet. The ceilings were high and tiered into three levels. The second tier had backlighting that lit the level above it. The walls were a lavender color. The king-size bed had an intricately carved, dark-stained wood headboard and footboard, with carvings of a balcony scene with witches and sword fighting that seemed to tell of a romance. Sammy rekindled his disdainful memories of high school Shakespeare. He peered out two large double doors near the bed that led to a patio that looked out onto a formal garden and fountain similar to the fountain in the front of the house. He used his gloved hands to rummage through two plain-looking side tables and found nothing of interest. He saw a family portrait resting on one of the side tables that looked to be a recent photo of the smiling husband and wife and their two children, a boy and a girl.

"Boss, do you want to see the son and mother?" George asked, interrupting Sammy's thought.

"Where is the girl?" Sammy asked.

"What do you mean?"

He showed him the picture, pointing to the girl. "Do we know where she is, and did you look in her room?"

"I saw the girl's room, but I forgot to ask the housekeeper about her. Her room was empty."

"We need to know where she is. Let's look in the son's room, and then we can give her a call."

"OK."

"And, George, we are the police officers. I know this is a strange and scary crime scene, something you don't come across in these parts, but you need to be the guy who steps away. The guy who parses out the information and does not let the scene obscure the data collection."

"Got it, sir," George said and followed Sammy to the son's room.

They walked down the hall, past the father's corpse, and entered the room through the open door. The scene was like a life-sized diorama.

"This is interesting," Sammy said.

"Not so for them, I guess," George said softly.

"This is a moment captured in time," Sammy said in awe and crouched down to closely inspect the woman. She was wearing a full-length blue night-gown. Her long, straight brown hair was worn behind her ears. She was kneeling, her hands clasped in prayer, about halfway down the length of the bed where her son was lying. Her angelic appearance was interrupted by dried blood at the nasal corners of her eyes and from her left nostril. Her son's eyes were closed and a dried red tear was present at the corner of his eye. The pale child looked pre-packaged for his funeral with a peaceful grin on his face and folded hands on his stomach.

"You know, George, I really don't know what I'm looking at here. We need the state crime lab to look at this."

"I'm surprised that you are stumped, boss."

"Well, even a veteran can get—"

Pffft. The handheld radio clipped to Sammy's belt went off, and he looked down at it.

It was Joe. "Captain, we need you down here quick. You have to see this." Pffft.

"Enough with the suspense. What do you have?" Sammy said.

"It's a girl, and she looks pretty bad." Pffft.

"Well, call the EMTs now. George and I are coming down. Does she need CPR?"

"She breathing on her own but looks like she is bleeding from her nose."

"Whatever you and Lenny do, do not touch her. Where are you, anyway?" Sammy asked as he and George ran down the ornate staircase.

"We're back in the cabana." Pffft.

Sammy and George reached the first floor and ran to the kitchen, where they flung open the back door. They sprinted toward the shed with all their gear jingling and jangling with each stride. They saw the open sliding door of the cabana. A girl, looking very pale and wearing a green one-piece bathing suit, was lying between Joe and Lenny, who were both crouched by her side. The girl moved her head back and forth, but her eyes were tightly shut. A fresh drop of blood came from her nose. Sammy put the back of his gloved hand on her forehead.

"She's burning up. Lenny, find a sink in here, and get her a glass of water," Sammy said. "Joe, what's the status of the ambulance?"

Joe was still staring at her. "They're on their way."

Sammy crouched beside Joe and the girl. He gently shook her right shoulder. "Hey, young lady, what's going on? What's bothering you? Where are you? What's your name?"

She only moaned in response and kept shaking her head as if she was trying to dislodge something in her hair.

"George, did you catch what the girl's name was when we were in the house?" Sammy asked.

"Virginia, Valerie? Uh, Valencia." George fumbled for her name.

"You sure?" Sammy asked.

"I'm positive," he said, his voice wavering.

"Well, let's give it a try," Sammy said.

"Valencia, dear. Valencia, if you can hear me, tell me what's going on. What is bothering you?" Sammy asked.

She moaned in answer.

Lenny ran toward them from the inside with a glass of water.

"Valencia, can you sit up, dear? We have some water. Are you thirsty?" Sammy wanted to lift the back of her head, but seeing as she was "found down," he was uncertain if she had broken any part of her spine. He took the glass from Lenny.

She still did not answer.

Sammy grabbed a towel that was hanging on a nearby fence and started dabbing her forehead with the water. Fresh blood continued to trickle from her nose.

"What?" she whispered. She kept her eyes closed.

"Hey, Valencia, this is police chief Sammy. You are at home. It's nearly noon. When did you come out here to the pool?" He babied her as if she was a lost child on a playground.

She went back to moaning.

The group heard the advancing sirens of the ambulance that stopped as the ambulance entered the circular drive, and the officers saw two EMTs get out, one male and one female, carrying a backboard and what looked like an orange tackle box.

"Hey, guys, what's going on?" the female EMT asked the group. The male EMT felt Valencia's breath with his cheek, felt her carotid pulse, and took her blood pressure.

"She was found down. Three others inside are dead. We can't tell the cause, but they all look like her. They have blood coming from their noses. She's burning up. I don't know if we are looking at a poisoning or an infection," Sammy told the rescuers.

"Sixty over palp, and she is tachycardic," the female EMT said. "Let's start an IV," she told her partner. "Do we have a name for her?"

"Valencia," Sammy said.

The female EMT crouched down. She opened Valencia's eyelids. Her sclerae were bright red all the way to her pupils. "Valencia, sweetie, my name is Joyce. I'm an EMT. Can you talk to me?"

Valencia didn't respond.

"Valencia, dear, Greg is starting an IV in your arm now. It's going to pinch. Don't be afraid. We are going to get you to a hospital."

Sammy, George, and Joe stood up from Valencia's side. Sammy motioned to Lenny to come close as well. Joyce, the female EMT, began speaking on her radio to the local emergency room. Meanwhile, after Greg placed the IV, he began to do some rudimentary neurological tests to assess whether

Valencia could feel her legs. After the assessment, they rolled her to one side and put the backboard on the ground beside her. They rolled her onto the backboard and strapped her in tightly. The police officers watched as they brought her to the ambulance.

"Does she have any next of kin? She's a child. We'll need to know if she was taking medications and to give permission for any procedures," Joyce said.

"As I said before, we have three dead relations in the house. Mend is her last name. We do have a housekeeper. If she can help, we will bring her. Where are you taking her?" Sammy asked.

"We will bring her to Indiana West to stabilize her, but the ER doctor there wants to send her to Indianapolis Children's. The chopper will be meeting us there."

They loaded her into the ambulance. Greg jumped in the back. Joyce closed the back and climbed into the front of the ambulance. They turned on their sirens and drove out of the Mend compound. The police officers looked on.

"Lenny, call up the state boys, and let them know to send their lab out here. Joe, you go out to talk to Miss Sanchez. George and I will follow the ambulance and then drive to Children's."

Chapter 2

"**I cannot keep** up this company. You have been groomed for this moment," Alejandro Mendosa said to his son. He sat comfortably back in a rich-brown leather nailhead chair. He was wearing a white button-down shirt and gray pants. His legs were crossed, and he bounced his free leg, awaiting his son's answer. A one-sided smile shone on his face. In his lap, he folded his hands on top of a small paunch. It was as if he knew his son's answer. For him, the hook was firmly in the fish's mouth, and despite the struggles of the fish, all that fisherman Mendosa needed was to reel him on board.

"What? No, Dad. You still have a lot of good years," John Mend said with deep, dark, pleading eyes. John knew why his father had called him. He had thought the time for this talk would still be in the future. He still wanted to make his own name and his own fortune. He still thought he could become the next young entrepreneur, even though he was at the outer edge of the age for a young Internet entrepreneur. His thin figure paced about the room.

"There is no need to be nervous about this. It's not like I am going to dump this on you and leave. I will mentor you for a year or so, and then you will run the show. The reasons I am doing this are for you to be the innovator that I can no longer be." Mendosa tried to reason with him. He knew that his son had wanted to be his own man for a long time.

"How is that? This is your agricultural company. You created it. You made it great," John said, somewhat forcefully.

"I am likely to die with the company, Juan, if it keeps going the way it's going," his father said, referring to John by his Spanish birth name. "I hybridize plants with cross-pollination. The other big companies, they are splicing and dicing genes. They are using Internet algorithms to tailor the seeds to each individual farmer. The other companies grease the correct palms to get exclusivity to their projects."

John finally sat down. "Then you should do what they do and do it better."

"That's not my way of doing things. I work with small farmers. I understand their needs. I work with hybridists to improve on products that are in the marketplace. I shake hands with customers and suppliers, and I grease my palms when I work on the tractor that I use to go out in the experimental fields."

"You must change, then."

"I'm an old fellow who knows his limitations and who knows what is good for his own investments. Unfortunately, I'm a tortoise in a field of hares."

"Doesn't the tortoise win in the end?" John looked at him in puzzlement.

"In this race, I'd get turned into turtle soup," Mendosa said dryly.

"Why me? Why not Jorge?"

"Your brother, have you seen him lately? He's an artist. A part-time longshoreman and fisherman. I send someone to check on him, because he doesn't want to talk to me. Bah. My two children, why do you run away from me?" Mendosa said, with cupped hands.

"What, what do you mean?" John said, completely clueless.

"You." Mendosa smirked. "Maybe I misjudged your intelligence. You have completely severed family association and legacy and have been transformed into the unique, totally unattached being that is John Mend. Who is that?"

"It was your fault. I mean, it was meant to be a compliment. I mean, you made your own multimillion-dollar company on your own two feet. How was I to do that on my own? I knew as a small boy that I wanted to be like you. Then as a teenager I still felt that way, but I didn't want to be you. I wanted people to know that I earned what I got on my own. Not because of my rich dad."

"I know this is sudden. If I go, then I will turn over the company to the board or sell it off. Is that what you would like me to do? Do you have the next big idea? Right now you are toiling in a little company run by others. You're getting older, and just like they do with me, the new kids are lapping you in innovation."

"Hmph," John said and rolled his eyes. He was in his late twenties, but he didn't like the idea of his father calling him a has-been.

"You think on it. Think about how smart you are and how much you could add to this business—your family business. Think about how much time you have wasted not being the next big innovator. Think about how your special talents can help this company survive. And not only that, thrive." Mendosa stood up and put his hand on his son's shoulder. He then walked out of the room.

John put his face in his hands and stayed in the chair for a moment. He looked around the room at the dark mahogany walls and the large desk with carved legs. The tops of the legs were etched with heads of roaring lions, like the crest of Spain. He thought of the magnitude of the office. The ability to move such a large net worth with an order or stroke of a pen. Despite his belief that he could be his own entrepreneur, he wondered if he could handle this pressure. He wondered at the great fortune to be able to inherit a company like this.

He left the office and headed to his childhood bedroom. It had not been touched since he left it at the age of eighteen. Banners of the old New York and the newer San Francisco baseball Giants were on the walls. He had an eight-by-eleven signed, framed picture of Willie Mays swinging his bat. He laid face down on his bed, perpendicular to his pillow, with his feet hanging off the end of the bed. The memories of classmates came to him. Many of them had jobs waiting for them like the one he was about to inherit. He always thought he would be better than them and walk away from inheritance. He changed his name, took out loans, wore no label clothing, and drove a twenty-year-old car to hide from his wealthy background. He even "changed" his ethnicity to a Northern European Lutheran, to make sure others didn't see that he might be from a disadvantaged minority who would receive government assistance or politically correct corporate handouts.

While lying on his bed, he caught a glimpse of a shiny object on a side table beside his bed. He reached for it. The gold necklace he held had an image of the Virgin Mary, and on the back was a cross. This was his mother's jewelry. She gave this to him before she died. His mother had a rare cancer, and despite the family's means, they were unable to find a cure for her. He looked at the necklace and remembered her final days.

⋏

"I know you want to be your own man. I accept your change in name, and I know you want to go your own way. You know your father needed me so badly. He was like a wooden facade of a man. I was what propped him up from behind. When I'm gone, he'll have no backing. You need to listen to your father. Despite his various business successes, he knows he really has nothing without his family. You can still be your own man and take up his torch. Have you seen those runners who carry the Olympic torch? Each has his or her own story, and everyone in the world focuses on that individual story, and why we focus on that story is the gift of the torch. If your father wants you to take over the business, use it as your torch." His emaciated mother winced in pain after each sentence. She was lying in her bed at their home. After several years of chemotherapeutics in many of the country's top medical centers, she had decided to retreat from fighting her rare form of cancer.

"This agriculture business, Mom, is just not me. I don't want to do this. I want to make my own mark," he said, in a low, almost-whispering voice to her as if a louder tone alone would tip her into her grave.

She gripped his hand tightly with her bony hand. "I wanted more out of life, too. I will not hold my grandchildren. I wanted to see my sons settled. I wanted to see their successes. I wanted more for myself. But still I had a good life doing what I had to do and not what I wanted."

Her hand loosened in his as she started to fatigue, even from this short conversation. To John, the whole room seemed to have dimmed. Her eyes closed. The conversations of his father and brother talking with other family in the downstairs foyer percolated into his mother's bedroom. He wanted to say no and finish the conversation. His mother had not at this moment convinced him otherwise. But he did not have the courage to say no to someone who was a few moments from seeing the Almighty.

He let go of his mother's hand and walked out of the room. The next few days, his mother would start to go in and out of consciousness. Between his mother's lapses of cognition and hovering family, he was never able to broach the subject of his father's business with her again. Within a week she died, and with it their conversation, which he never told anyone else. He always felt that after she died, in moments of success at his Internet job, she was perched overhead with wishful eyes, hoping he would change his mind.

⅄

Now, several years after that event, lying on his bed, he sensed that his angel mother would be getting her wish. The feeling of "being behind the eight ball" crept inside him. He was already too late to be a boy Internet genius. Was he too late to take advantage of this opportunity? He hated giving up what had been his desired career, the one that he believed would make him happy. He saw the day in the future working in a career that he didn't want day in and day out, only to be struck down like his mother. He processed this for a moment and grabbed a swatch of comforter from his bed. He put it in his mouth and bit down hard. He flung his legs up and down. At the end of his tantrum, he shed a tear.

The next morning, he got up from his childhood bed, went into his father's office, and signed papers agreeing to take over his father's company, Quality Seed.

Chapter 3

"I don't know how we can compete," John Mend said to his chief scientist at the entryway of the chief's lab.

"You know the formula for success—we need a better-yielding, better-tasting product," Vivek Satchinanda said in a very thick accent. He went by simply Vivek to his peers. To his underlings he was Dr. Satchinanda, and if he liked you, Satch. He was thin and stood five feet six inches tall, with dark-brown skin and curly black hair, thinning at the temples. His well-trimmed mustache was nearly connected to horn-rimmed glasses, and these features hid almost all the rest of his face, including high cheekbones.

"Thank you, Vivek. I look to you to actually *help* me find some molecular solutions to our problems," John said sarcastically, leaning forward with both hands on a slate lab table.

"The markets are getting smaller and the competition more fervent. We have the nongenetically modified hybridized corn that we have been working on for years, and we have not come out with any breakthrough products. Our other genetically modified crops are doing somewhat well with at least as much, if not more, yield as the AgWorld products, but we have limited that to commercial feed, fuel production, and corn-syrup production." Dr. Satchinanda explained to John the self-created gaps between technology and the marketplace.

"I'm beginning to think GMO is the way for us to go." Mend sighed, with a bit of defeat in his eyes.

"I don't think your father would want to go about messing with crops for human consumption in that way. He did most of the early hybridizing of our edible crops. For industrial purposes and feed lots, genetically modified is fine, but for consumer use, I think it would be imprudent."

"It may be imprudent, but is it more imprudent to go out of business? If we are one of the good guys, we can say we are doing GMO the right way because we have been faithful to our customer base in giving them the highest-quality product. Besides, this is my company now." John pounded his fist on the slate table.

"I do not think the idea of being a thief who says 'please' counts as being a good guy." Dr. Satchinanda stood his ground.

John paced about the room. "Can we do better than GMO with our non-GMO hybridization techniques?"

"You know we make the best-tasting corn now."

"Yes, but at what yield? We cannot sustain this company on selling one ear of corn at a time, like some street-side vegetable stand."

"We have been incrementally increasing yield."

"Yes, at a snail's pace. While AgWorld is moving at light speed. The food industry is watching. From frozen food to chain restaurants, they want yield. They want yield so they can pay less," John explained.

"We have offered drought- and disease-resistant hybrids to our farmer customers, and that is who we sell to, not to the makers of TV dinners and rest-stop restaurants."

"That's who eventually gets it, so they are appealing to their customers. AgWorld has been doing this model for years."

"I do not think we should stoop to their level." Dr. Satchinanda stomped his foot.

"Well, I'll let you think about this overnight, Vivek. If we don't come up with a plan soon, this place will be boarded up or auctioned off. How would you like to be working for AgWorld again?"

Dr. Satchinanda remembered his months at AgWorld. So many business people and inferior scientists telling him what to do. People with MBAs telling him to move one nucleotide up or down to save some money in production costs. They cared very little about long-term safety, as long as their customers did not vomit or have diarrhea within seventy-two hours.

As soon as John left his lab, Dr. Satchinanda turned and walked to his office, which was attached to the lab. He wondered if this was just another one of John's motivational speeches to get the lab to work harder. He had encountered these walk-ins from John mostly after board meetings. John would come in at the end of the corporate day and let him know where things were going wrong. Unfortunately, he never heard when things were going right. The pace of progress kept the scientists and technicians uncomfortable. Throughout the years, he and his fellow scientists had built up the GMO production of corn but only for the "bulk" products he mentioned to John in the meeting. The corn that would be eaten in whole or partial form was always non-GMO. The belief had been that what made Mend's Quality Seed company a great and profitable institution was the natural way their edible-corn breeds were made.

The techniques for making the non-GMO corn was a longer process of trial and error that was not that different from experiments conducted by the monk and father of genetics, Gregor Mendel. Despite Quality Seed's manual manipulation, it was deemed natural, as it was quite possible that in nature a pollinator like a bee might interact with two plants to make an ideally tasting one. After all, what we see as corn today started out as a grass that Native Americans hybridized for years.

This meeting with John was different, as the movement toward human-consumed GMO compromised the one area where Quality Seed remained pure, and the movement would abandon the company's history and identity. Dr. Satchinanda dwelt on this reality and wondered if it was worth it. The alternative to not genetically altering their human-edible crop could be the sale of the company and the eventual dismantling of the natural crop, anyway. He wondered if there was a third way, a way to possibly get the characteristics without changing the genes. He left his office at the end of the day still mulling this over.

After his usual one-hour commute, he arrived at the two-story cookie-cutter developer's dream home. All the homes in his neighborhood looked similar, with little variation, and had large two-car garages facing the street, which defined the appearance. The richness of spices greeted him when he opened his front door, tickling his nose and making him sneeze. Vivek Satchinanda walked into his kitchen to see his wife stirring away at *sambar,* an Indian stew made with lentils and vegetables. He could only see her back as she concentrated on making dinner by the stove. She wore a dark-red blouse with shiny sequins on the borders of her collar and blue jeans. Toward the back of the kitchenette, his oldest son and his twin daughters sat at a round, white wooden table.

The boy's focused eyes peered beyond chubby cheeks at a book on the table. His hair was long, and he kept blowing his bangs out of his face. "Stop it! I'm trying to work!" he shouted for a moment and then returned to his task. He was yelling at his younger sisters, who were fighting over a doll and agitating their brother.

"She took my doll," one of the girls said to her mother.

Vivek's wife looked up from her stirring of sambar and from the distance of the stove, said, "Both of you stop fighting. No dolls at the table. Your father is home, and it is time to eat. Ajay, stop your homework for now, and wash your hands for dinner."

His son put down his pencil and ran to the guest bathroom to wash up. The girls disregarded their mother and continued to fight for the doll underneath the table.

Lakshmi Satchinanda put the girls on hold for the moment. She held a tight reign over her children, and they, for the most part, listened to her. Her day job was as the manager of information technology for a local hospital. She was as brilliant as her husband, and they made a good team. After commanding the children, she spun around, and as if on cue, she kissed Dr. Satchinanda on the cheek.

"How was your day?" she asked.

"Another one of those board tantrums I had to hear about from John," Dr. Satchinanda answered as he walked. He put his work bag down on top of Ajay's homework and sat at the table, facing his twin daughters. They smiled at him as a cover for the little war they were having over the doll. He barely acknowledged the smile, since he was still dwelling on what was usually the mundane question of "How was work?"

"That does not seem like anything new," Lakshmi said as she doled out rice, sambar, and spiced okra on shiny metal plates for the children and her husband. She passed the full plates to her husband first and then to each of the children. Lastly, she prepped a plate for herself and sat down at the table.

"I don't like this food," one of girls said and scrunched up her face in disgust.

"Your mother spent a lot of time making this food. You should eat it," Dr. Satchinanda said.

"I want spaghetti, Mommy," her sister whined.

"No! Who will eat your rice and sambar? Huh! If you go to India, you will see plenty of children without rice and sambar!" Dr. Satchinanda started to raise his voice. His family back home in India was relatively well to do and had businesses and worked for the Indian government's various bureaus. But he remembered the hundreds of emaciated beggars dressed in rags, holding their hands out in search of coins or sustenance. Vivek shook his head at his children's ungratefulness for their current station.

Ajay barely took notice of the argument and busily ate his rice. He was in his early teens, and, other than video games, his priority was eating. Because his sisters were his sisters and much younger siblings, he didn't mind if they got a good tongue-lashing.

"OK, now, everybody, calm down," Lakshmi said as she started to get up from her chair. "I have some *idlis* in the fridge that you can have, as long as you have some sambar and vegetables." She walked to the fridge and grabbed a few of the white circular cakes made from black lentils and rice and warmed them in the microwave.

Dr. Satchinanda gave his daughter an angry look as his wife served them their idlis. He was not one to let minor infractions to his sensibilities fade from his memory.

"What? At least they are eating. You don't know how hard it is to feed these two," Lakshmi said, responding to his gaze. She tapped him on the back to snap him out of his vengeance.

The remainder of the dinner was quiet, as the girls first asked to be excused, and a few moments later, with his cheeks still full of food, Ajay joined their egress. The girls ran upstairs to their bedroom to fight over dolls. Ajay returned to his homework, interspersed with video games.

The remainder of the night went as usual. Vivek started scrubbing plates and then putting them in the dishwasher, keeping his mind off work with drudgery. He eventually made it upstairs, brushed his teeth, and changed into his pajamas, which were dark blue with a button-down front. He lay in bed face up, with his multicolored, multipatched quilt pulled to his chest. In the distance, he could hear Lakshmi in the family prayer room, in what sounded like a beautiful bird cadence.

After prayers, Lakshmi tucked the girls in and still gave Ajay a peck on the forehead at night. Lakshmi came into their bedroom and began changing for bed. She looked at his statuesque appearance. He looked to her like the cover art of an Egyptian sarcophagus. "What are you thinking about? The stupid board meeting?"

"Yes," he said tersely.

"Do you want to talk about it? Do you have any options?"

"No and maybe."

Lakshmi turned off the light and gave him a kiss on the cheek. He seemed too distant in thought to get much more affection. She left him in his sarcophagal position.

He didn't stay there for long when the lights went out. He moved from his left side and then to his right. He lay on his stomach and rubbed his feet together. He crouched in the fetal position. The haphazard movements in bed correlated to the struggle he was having in his mind. Unfortunately, he kept drawing closer and closer to an answer he really did not want to find. He dreamed of a molecular biology convention in Las Vegas fifteen years ago.

⚓

"Hey, buddy, you got a light?" asked an unshaven man with blond hair parted in the middle. He wore a leather jacket.

"This is a lecture hall. They don't let you smoke in here. Please be quiet. I am trying to listen to the lecture," Dr. Satchinanda said sternly. He would normally have sat up front, but ended up in the back row as he needed to ask the previous lecturer a question. The conference of the Plant Genome Society was so poorly organized. The large, airport-like convention center had convention-goers ping-ponging nearly half a mile to different lecturers that were spaced a mere five minutes apart.

The lecturer was from the Boston Plant Institute, and he was describing the process of introducing proteins into plants to make them stronger and heartier. The room was very dark. About fifty scientists were in the room. Dr. Satchinanda listened attentively, as his company, AgWorld, was trying to make a genetically modified soybean.

The grizzly bearded man with his unlit cigarette in his mouth leaned over to Dr. Satchinanda's ear and touching his shoulder, said, "You know he is full of shit."

"He is one of the foremost experts in the field. I highly doubt, sir, that your acumen in this field rivals his." He could smell alcohol on the man's breath. He saw rings under his eyes. The man was probably a jealous researcher who'd never published or done as well as the speaker. Dr. Satchinanda started to look for another seat away from this man.

"His data works in the lab but not on the street. He's an academic who doesn't have the pressures we have in the commercial lab. He's not like one of us. I've done this work in rice for my company. We got the yield, but unfortunately it wouldn't last."

The man must have seen Dr. Satchinanda's personalized folder from AgWorld. "Excuse me," he said to the annoying man and abruptly stood up. He found a seat on the other side of the row. Vivek looked down the row to see if the scruffy rogue scientist cared about his departure. An attractive brunet woman took Dr. Satchinanda's former seat. He saw the know-it-all with his left arm around the back of the woman's chair. The man caught Dr. Satchinanda's eye, smirked at him, and gave him a two-fingered salute. Dr. Satchinanda frowned and focused on the lecture.

After the lecture, Dr. Satchinanda had some downtime before the next talk. He sat in an atrium with numerous chairs and tables and looked over the program for the rest of the day. The breeze of fellow scientists who walked close by lifted the light pages of the program in front of him. Their footsteps squeaked on the well-polished floor. It was good white noise for concentration. A lot of information was presented at the conference, and any assistance to aid in the digestion of the material was a great help. He gazed at the notes of the previous lecturer and was entranced by the information. The data all looked accurate and applicable to his own work, and he didn't understand what the obnoxious stranger was referring to as "inaccurate." A few minutes went by, and a set of squeaky steps seemed to stall behind him. He looked up from the notes.

"His data looks even worse on paper than on the lecture screen." It was the scruffy man with the beard who smelled of cigarettes and alcohol. His hands were in his jeans pockets, and he was hovering over Dr. Satchinanda's shoulder.

Dr. Satchinanda looked at him over the top rims of his glasses in irritation. He was a bit afraid of saying anything to him, as it might incite a conversation. He was never one to attract "strays," and he always believed that he needed to start up the conversation with known or unknown people, as they usually ignored him. "Why do you keep saying this?"

"Because as I said, I've done this myself in my own lab." He had come around to one of the chairs next to Dr. Satchinanda and pulled it back. The chair let out a screech as it rubbed against the floor.

"And who are you to say this?"

"I'm Barry Orr, and I work for Reliable Agriculture. We're out of Elkhart, Indiana," Barry said and blew the long blond hair out of his face.

"Never heard of your company."

"We're a little start-up. As I mentioned in the lecture, I've done this work and done it better than this guy." Barry smirked and reached into his jacket pocket and pulled out a rolled brochure. He handed it to Dr. Satchinanda.

Dr. Satchinanda took a brisk look at the brochure, primarily at the pictures. The glossy brochure was advertising for investors. The pictures showed smiling scientists working in laboratories and the most basic lay definition of molecular genetics. Graphs and tables of product lines and potential profits were placed at the end of the booklet. Dr. Satchinanda put the fairly worn brochure on the table. "Looks like a nice little outfit. So if you are so smart, why don't you give the lecture?"

"Yeah, I'm sure your buddies at AgWorld would like me to be handing them our corporate secrets left and right."

"Is that what you're trying to get from me?" Dr. Satchinanda asked with some concern.

"There is no useful information to get from your large, bumbling, bureaucratic company. I worked there before, and I know you have no secrets worth sharing," Barry said, smiling.

"You did? When and with whom?" Dr. Satchinanda was curious, as he never remembered seeing this man in the lab.

"A few years back in a postdoctoral position. I was trying to get myself established in the company, but I ended up as chief bottle washer. I gleaned things on my own in Bart Berg's lab, dealing with sorghum genes. He was trying to make it less appetizing to birds."

"Never heard of him," Dr. Satchinanda said and hoped this would end the conversation. It was not altogether surprising that he would not know who Dr. Berg was. AgWorld was a large Fortune 500 corporation that employed thousands of scientists. He looked back down at his lecture notes.

"You know you shouldn't stay there." Barry got close to his face.

"Why? Are you trying to recruit me?" Dr. Satchinanda replied to his notes and not to Barry.

"I like my position. I think you'd be taking my job. You seem to like your work. AgWorld doesn't let you do that. Management will work you hard and destroy your imagination. You are not an individual to them. You are either a dollar sign or an easily replaceable number to them. They will take away your creativity and your ideas in the name of the 'corporation.' They will take it all away from you."

"You don't know me. Why would you talk to me about this? You don't even know my name." Dr. Satchinanda lifted his head and looked at him annoyed, as he could feel Barry's breath on his face.

"I dunno. Just feel like it." Barry smiled and shrugged his shoulders.

Dr. Satchinanda took his glasses off and rubbed his forehead in irritation. He wondered why this man was toying with him, as if he was a ball of yarn tossed back and forth by a kitten.

"You're right. I don't know you. What did you say your name was?" Barry asked.

"Ugh." Dr. Satchinanda groaned under his breath with the conflict in his head. He wanted this pest to go away. He was scared of the consequences of letting Barry know his identity, but he also thought he would find out, anyway, through the convention-attendance directory. "My name is Vivek Satchinanda."

"Well, Satch, I'd say you'd be better off with John Mend's Quality Seed Company."

"First of all, I said, 'Satchinanda.' And now you are giving me life advice."

"Satch, as in Satchmo, Louis Armstrong, the jazz musician. That, to me, sounds pretty cool. Second of all, Mend's got a great company and sounds like he would let you have the run of the place. You could get things done and see results of your scientific research right away. Right on the streets. If I can save one of my fellow scientists from the brain-beating juggernaut of AgWorld, I'd be happy to do so," Barry said joyfully.

"Well, if it is such a good opportunity, why didn't you take it?"

"I tried. I don't think Mr. Mend cares for my antics." Barry smiled.

"Antics?"

"Hey, Satch, speaking of which." Barry looked at his watch. "Looks like we can get a matinee at Slick Sam's. I have a wad of ones that need to find a home in a G-string."

"It is twelve thirty in the afternoon. There are several more lectures to attend. Why did you even come to the conference if you either do not believe the speakers or do not attend the lectures?" Dr. Satchinanda said and began to get up from his chair.

"C'mon, this is Las Vegas. That was the only reason I came here. So do you want to go?" Barry said, pleading with his new friend.

"I'm a happily married man, and it's time for the next lecture." Dr. Satchinanda stepped away from his chair.

Barry held out his arm, impeding Dr. Satchinanda's departure. In his hand was a business card. "Hey, Satch, take my card. Just in case you need some friendly advice or a drinking buddy."

Dr. Satchinanda took the card, stood up, and said, "I don't drink."

Barry sat in Dr. Satchinanda's chair and put his feet up on a nearby table. He buried his chin in his chest and closed his eyes.

Dr. Satchinanda noticed this and trepidatiously asked, "I thought you were going somewhere?"

"Nah, I don't want to go by myself. I think I'll take a nap and then have a few drinks at the convention bar when it opens," Barry said, with his eyes closed.

Dr. Satchinanda walked away without saying good-bye.

A year later he remembered that conversation. It was a long day in the lab, and a young manager, a tall, young, good-looking fellow with high cheekbones and a receding hairline had come in, yelling at him about not meeting a deadline. The entire time the manager was berating him, he thought of his conversation with Barry and how empty his career had been. He had very little input with AgWorld and was regularly admonished for not having data ready for managers. This had little to do with Dr. Satchinanda's skill but the nature of how scientific procedures took place. This fact was irrelevant to the managers and particularly to the one who was in his face. After the manager left, he made a call to John Mend and within a few months was working for Quality Seed.

Now many years later, John Mend had started to sound like the AgWorld manager. There was, however, a helpless, less-demeaning quality to his conversation, as Mend knew well the limitations of the science. Dr. Satchinanda tossed and turned in bed, thinking about asking Barry to bail out Quality Seed. Barry was such an odd and uncouth man and in many ways very arrogant. That arrogance, though, could help in creating some scientific breakthroughs, as he wouldn't accept establishment limitations. He struggled with the idea of calling him, not only due to his odd personality but because of the possibility that he could lose his job if Barry somehow took over. Dr. Satchinanda was not a molecular geneticist like Barry, and currently about half the crops coming from Quality Seed were genetically modified. If the remainder of the products were genetically modified as well, he would be obsolete. The last ten years at Quality Seed had been some of the best scientific and personal years of his life, and he did not want to see that end. He came to the conclusion that he wanted the best for his company and his boss, who had made his life so happy in the preceding decade. In the morning, he decided to talk to John about calling Barry and letting John decide with all the facts laid out.

Chapter 4

"Not bad," Eric Feldberg said. His tie was loosened at his collar, top button undone. He had just come home after a long day of meetings. His forearms were on the end of the table. One hand held a fork, and the other had a knife. He talked with his mouth full.

"I'm glad you like it. I had Ayanna make the enchiladas mild, the way you like it," his wife, Melissa, said. She sighed afterward. She was wearing a white blouse. Her long, blond, nearly white hair was draped over her right shoulder. Her legs were crossed, and a glossy-black, heeled shoe bounced up and down nervously on her one knee. She wore very bright red lipstick to contrast her very white skin.

"Thanks for doing that, Melissa." Eric looked at a paper on the table.

"Do you mind not doing that?" she asked in a pleading voice. At this moment, she wanted a family moment and at least a conversation with her husband that she never saw and barely talked to.

"What?" Eric was surprised, as the request had never been made before. He was the proverbial king of his castle, and he came and went and did as he pleased for much of their marriage.

"Can you put that paper down? This is the one time we get to see each other and talk."

A baby cooed between them.

"All right. Well, how is the little lady doing?"

"If you mean Annabelle, she is doing fine. Ayanna took her on a little walk around the park."

Eric put his index finger in the little girl's hand. She giggled and kicked her feet in her little high chair. "Da, da, da, da."

"I want to go back to work," she said, with a piercing glare.

"OK by me," Eric said nonchalantly. He didn't particularly care what she did with herself, as long as it did not interfere with him.

"I can't really sit around here doing nothing. Ayanna takes care of Annabelle and the house. I sit around and do nothing. Maybe I have a drink at noon. I get to read a lot."

"I said OK," he said more sternly, only to get her off the topic. He honestly did not care how she spent her days, as long as it didn't embarrass him or cost him money. All day he had to make decisions about AgWorld, and he didn't want to make decisions for her.

"I'm glad you approve," she said coldly. She wanted more of an answer. Essentially she was looking for him to care or for her to matter to him. She wanted an answer with a principle behind it to show that he cared about her and their relationship. The answer he gave her to what was for her a monumental decision was the same as he would have given if she told him she was having steak for dinner. She wouldn't have minded if he'd said no, as long as he reasoned a connection between them and their relationship, as if it was relevant.

"This conversation is better than me reading the paper?"

"I wish you would take an interest in my daily life. Some days I don't think you care what I do. I could be flushing all your money down the toilet. You wouldn't care." Her voice increased in volume with each sentence.

"Do you ask me about my day?" he asked calmly, challenging her suppositions.

"Well, how was your day?" she said, snapping each syllable of her words, with her leg feverishly bouncing on her knee.

"Fine," he said bluntly.

She kept staring at him, waiting for more, waiting for an emotion other than anger. She had been questioning their relationship for some time, even before the birth of Annabelle. The couple had met five years prior at a black-tie soiree for executives and executive "hangers-on." Eric was a rising star at AgWorld, but one couldn't tell; he acted as if he was already the chief executive of the company. He was standing with younger vice presidents and managers from other companies from various different industries. She suspected executives of his own company feared his confidence. That confidence drew her to him. At the time, she was an interior designer for a large firm in Chicago. She liked her career but did not feel fulfilled. She wanted more, she wanted something lasting, and she wanted a family. Her father passed away when she was a child. Her mother and sisters were not close and were scattered in the Southeast and Southwest. Her longest relationship had ended five years before, and since then she had been in transient relationships. Eric appeared in control of his surroundings, which she felt she did not have. He had control she hoped would translate to caring. They dated for a year before getting married. He didn't want to be tied down. She tried hard to convince him that he would be the boss of his realm, and she would only bask in his kingdom. Only in the last year did she realize that being his serf didn't mean caring, but she felt stuck. At this point, she wanted a more active life of her own to forget feeling trapped.

Melissa, leaving her half-eaten dinner, picked up Annabelle. "I'm going to put her to bed, and then I'm going to bed."

"Sounds like a plan. I'll be up in a few hours. I want to take a look at some things before I hit the sack." He smiled a fake smile at her. He knew that ignoring her was the best way to get her off his back. He had no doubt that he was the alpha male of the family, and whatever he said or did would go.

Melissa stood for a moment, looking at him, with Annabelle on her shoulder. The baby girl tucked her face in her mother's ear. Without any response from Eric, she stormed off to the nursery.

Eric stared off into the skyline out of their expansive, floor-to-ceiling glass windows and thought of his father. His father taught him chess. He also told him to do with his life what he wanted as he preached to him that life was short. The elder taught him to be the master of his own universe and to move the planet chess pieces to his own whim. His father was a man of his word and lived his life according to what he taught young Eric. Throughout his childhood he saw this hardworking man at the stock brokerage, trying to climb his way to the top of his firm. One of the ways he climbed up the social ladder was to have lavish cigar and scotch parties with coworkers when Eric was a child, and all the children would run between the legs of happily inebriated adults. At the same time, he was able to have as much glee during off hours, where he would watch baseball with his kids. He even kept up to date with all the players on all the teams, even their minor-league stats.

Eric remembered the most profound event in his life, which occurred during his fourteenth birthday party. The party was in a big hall filled to capacity with adults and kids. His father purchased an open bar that all the teens and tweens tried to partake in. They were disappointedly turned away. At the end of the festivities, as he and his friends started to disperse, he asked his mother where his father was. She clutched him painfully by the arm, her nails digging under his bicep, and said, "He took Aunt Agnes home. He is not coming home with us tonight."

Aunt Agnes was an attractive woman who came to the cigar and scotch parties in tight, low-cut dresses. She had a small but very obvious shiny cross that hung in her cleavage. He thought she was unique because of this pendant, as most of their friends were Jewish like them or nonreligious or, at least, nonadvertising Christians. He often wondered how odd it was that his father and Aunt Agnes acted so playfully with one another. Through his mother's death grip and screeching answer, he knew that Aunt Agnes was his father's mistress. His father was able to have it all: a great job, a family, a wife, and a mistress. He controlled all these pieces.

What his father could not control was an IRS audit of the company that essentially broke their family. Eric hated the government as their finances turned upside down. Within months of his father's audit, his mother filed for divorce. In college, he would go to pubs with the disheveled, divorced, and mistressless father. Gone were the days of cigar and scotch parties. Eric pushed away his plate at the dinner table and noticed how much he was like his father at the pinnacle of his career. Unlike his father, he thought of controlling the government and harnessing it for his use instead of being blindsided by it.

This was one of the few moments of retrospection he allowed himself to have. For Eric, relying on the past was a weakness, and thinking about it was a hindrance to future success. He stared out the window at the various skyscrapers. One building was a rook, one was a knight, and another was a bishop. They were all to be manipulated and taken.

Chapter 5

Y**ou're hogging the** mirror," Daisy Montblanc's voice snipped.

"Ah, I was here first. And besides, the interviewers will be talking to me," Jessica Freeman said. She was a light-skinned African American woman whose very light complexion was adorned with teeny freckles surrounding her nose. Her hair had long, bouncy curls. She was a woman in her early thirties, but in the right outfit, she could pass for a sixteen-year-old. At the moment, she was trying to get her makeup done to make her look more mature.

"Fine. I'll use the downstairs bathroom," Daisy said huffily and stomped down the stairs. The stairs creaked as she made her way down the narrow passage. The old row home in the Capitol Hill district of Washington, DC, had these occasional eccentricities.

They were like this before all the big events. The couple would snip at each other and act like teen sisters preparing for a big dance. They worked for one of the largest nongovernmental organizations (NGOs) against genetically modified foods. NOGMO was the largest NGO, with nearly fifty million members, many of whom were based on social-media "likes" and not necessarily donations. In the realm of the NGO, they held some weight in political decisions. Jessica would personally lobby members of Congress or the White House to limit the use and sale of genetically modified foods. When she was unable to influence legislators, they had a small army of attorneys, who were ready to argue their positions. NOGMO wanted no genetically modified organisms on the planet. The organization's core belief was that genetically modified organisms cause harm to those organisms that eat them and then also have downstream effects on the environment. Diseases that GMO organisms can cause were numerous and quoted in the recent NOGMO pamphlet. NOGMO quoted small numbers of studies because only small numbers had been conducted. The ones available did not meet the gold standard of using double-blind procedures on individuals who either did or did not eat GMOs. This fact became the favorite excuse that legislators used to reject anti-GMO laws when confronted with groups like NOGMO.

Daisy stood in front of the guest bathroom, pulling the tangles from her hair. They both hated getting ready in this bathroom, as the fluorescent bulbs took forever to get to their full luminescence. During these petty fights, she would reassess her relationship with Jessica. They both were very independent, and at times it seemed that the small atoms of their relationship nucleus would split apart. Daisy took out her anger on the knots in her hair. She had long, wavy hair, and the process of combing allowed her to dwell on history.

Today, Daisy felt particularly disgruntled, but she didn't know why. She thought about a time twenty years ago on the family farm. She was one of many Montblanc grandchildren who visited the grand dame of Pennington plantation. Contrary to what the family suggested, the farm was not owned and tilled by them since the Revolution but was owned by another before them. After the War Between the States (as the Civil War was described in that area), the previous family was unable to maintain the farm without slaves or Confederate currency. The property was divided in two, with one hundred acres holding the antebellum home, sold over time to more recently become a townhome community, and the remaining two hundred sold to Steven Penn. A distant relative of William Penn, he changed his name to Montblanc to sound more regal and left his Quaker meeting house for a local Presbyterian church. As a sentiment to his previous name, he called the farm Pennington. Mr. Penn was a carpetbagger's carpetbagger and took full advantage of Mr. Levi's destitution during Reconstruction. He also took advantage of all the abundant labor once slavery ended, with near slave wages.

The home that Daisy's grandmother lived in was a great antebellum-style home built by her ancestor, Mr. Penn. The large Doric columns held up a two-story porch. Daisy remembered chatting with her grandmother on this first-floor porch in the spring of her senior year in high school. Gone was the nineteenth-century Philadelphia accent of her grandmother's ancestors; Grandma Montblanc's voice adopted the white southern drawl. Grandma had married a local assemblyman who died of a heart attack shortly after all her children were born.

"Don't listen to that father of yours," her grandmother said. What Grandma actually said defied much of the conservativism that would be assumed by outsiders in her accent. "You go on to that school up north, and do all the things I couldn't do."

At the time, she thought she was destined to be an environmental lawyer. The earth was in danger, and she was going to put a stop to all the pollutants with the power of the courts. When she was a small child, her father had wanted her to be a fair southern belle and carry on the Montblanc heritage. Her grades were too good to be another man's ornament, and her father began to think of her as the possible heir to his corporate law firm. Daisy's brother got along better with machines than people and was not in the running for law partner. By Daisy's senior year in high school, Mr. Montblanc had planned that she would go through undergrad and law school at Vanderbilt and possibly meet a nice boy who graduated from Virginia Military Institute. She would take over his Atlanta corporate law practice and Grandma's house and have a few grandkids, and they would be a big, happy southern family. Daisy had other plans. She didn't like her father's controlling nature, she was not particularly fond of money, and though Grandma's house was nice to visit, she liked it more for Grandma than the house.

She pulled another knot out of her hair, and her timeline moved forward as she sat in their little guest bathroom. The heat from the seven incandescent bulbs above the bathroom mirror was beginning to make doing her hair less bearable. Her memory traveled to the uncomfortable time when she brought home her then boyfriend Gilliam. This man she'd met at a coffee shop was white but had taken on the supposed persona of a Jamaican Rastafarian. He believed in all her justice causes, or at least she thought so between the grunts he purposed as speech. She remembered getting off the train coming from Boston and holding Gilliam's hand. The Amtrak was from Boston, as Vanderbilt had been out of the question, and she went to the more metropolitan Boston all-women's college for her studies.

When her father met Gilliam, he smelled the distinct odor of marijuana emanating from Gilliam's dreadlocks. Daisy remembered her father's usually pale complexion turning to a boiling red. Her father shook his hand tightly and received a limp limb in return. Mr. Montblanc shook his head. He tried one more time on the drive from the train station to his home to start a trivial conversation with Gilliam about sports—specifically, college football. He received Gilliam's usual barely audible grunt in response. With that, her father surrendered the house to her and Gilliam, making nanosecond appearances in between long hours at the office and golf course. Daisy would like to have seen her mother's laugh at Mr. Montblanc's reactions. Mrs. Montblanc, Daisy's mother, passed away from lung cancer when Daisy was a child, but before all eight months of what appeared to be pointless chemotherapy sessions, she always used to have a good laugh at the expense of her husband. In the end, Gilliam was one of Daisy's projects. She could never change him, and now years later, she thought he was either lazy, schizophrenic, not intelligent, or a combination of all three. After a nine-month relationship, she completely broke ties with Gilliam, much to her father's relief.

She was almost done with her hair and opened the window to let the cool air in to combat the heat from the lamps. The scent of a jasmine bush outside the window filled the small space. Daisy thought of how she met Jessica. She had had trysts with women before in her all-women's college. Bouncing between long-term relationships with men and short-term relationships with women, she vacillated with her sexual preferences. When she met Jessica at a party, she instantly was drawn to her. She loved her regimented personality and passion for legal advocacy. Not only that, Daisy wanted to bury her face in those curly locks. Daisy knew that with Jessica's dominant personality, she'd have to be subservient to Jessica and act like the needy men that she used to rescue. In recent times, Daisy felt as if she had become the helpless partner and yearned to be the "girl in charge."

A bee flew through the unscreened window and buzzed in Daisy's ear. "Ahhhh!" she screamed and ran her hands through her hair to get rid of the insect. She was always afraid of getting stung by a bee, though she had never been stung by one.

"What the hell is going on down there? Are you ready to go?" Jessica asked from upstairs.

Daisy did not respond right away. She looked in the mirror, and the time she'd spent doing her hair was, in a moment, wasted in a fit of bee swatting. She walked into the living room and saw a white straw cowboy hat on the coat rack, and she grabbed it and firmly plunked it on her head.

Jessica walked down the steps and saw Daisy looking at herself in the coatroom mirror. She was directly behind Daisy, so that she could see her. She raised an eyebrow. "Seriously?"

"What?" Daisy asked.

"It's a good thing that I'll be the one being interviewed," Jessica said curtly. A media presence would be at the fundraising event.

The couple walked out the door and headed toward the rally.

Chapter 6

The Amsterdam convention center was like an airplane hangar. The metal structure arched high above all the meeting attendees. John Mend walked up and down the aisles of scientific posters of geneticists. The posters were not particularly well organized. He was a bit frustrated that he could not find the genetics and transfection section. Once he found the section, he became distraught that it was primarily animal-based research. John looked at his phone-book-sized abstract manual and looked for the poster and scientist attached to the display. Number 653—there it was. He looked up from the manual and found a huddled group of scientists in front of the display.

John thought he would have to fight through a throng of scientists to get a word in with this scientist. He walked through a group of men of different ethnicities, who all seemed to wear metal-rimmed glasses and tweed jackets with patches on the elbows. The poster onlookers stared at him cautiously, as if they thought they would be pounced on by a would-be laboratory-supply representative. John was put together from his hair to his shoes, much like many of the salesmen parked a few hundred feet away in a separate area from the posters. He was relieved to see that the scientists were actually in front of poster number 655.

John walked up to a somewhat young-looking East Asian man with his long-on-top hair brushed to the side. The nervous and sweaty fellow was wearing an orange linen shirt, blue jeans, and brown sandals. He stared at

John and swallowed every few seconds, making his Adam's apple hop up and down.

John scanned the poster headline: THE NOVEL USE OF A NATIVE VIRUS ON RICE YIELDS. ORR, B. PHD, CHAN, F. MBBS. UNIVERSITY OF WESTERN KANSAS A&M.

"Hmm." John stared at the data. He knew some genetics, but he left the advanced genetics to Dr. Satchinanda. He looked at the young man and back at the two names claiming authorship of the poster. He had never met Dr. Orr and did not have a physical description of him. Dr. Satchinanda had told John to keep a low profile until he could figure out if he wanted to be associated with the scientist at all. Dr. Orr was, in Satchinanda's words, a "loose cannon" in regards to his professional and personal demeanor, and any relationship that Quality Seed formed with him should be tethered. John wanted to set up an interview with Orr in Indiana, but Orr, through Satchinanda, said that John should meet him here. This way John could hobnob with other agricultural company execs and possibly find other better scientists to do the experiments at Quality Seed. It seemed odd that an accomplished scientist would use such a self-defeatist statement for a job interview, but Satchinanda assured John that Orr was the scientist he needed to get the job done. With this in mind, John sized up the anxious fellow beside the poster.

"Is this your poster?" John asked.

"Yes," the fellow said and bowed.

"What do you think the cost would be to do this on a commercial scale?"

"Uh…" he said, stammering. "I don't know total cost for supplies for our experiment. Dr. Orr would be the best source of information," he said in his best broken English.

"Are you Dr. Chan?" he asked, hoping not to offend, though he had no physical description of Dr. Orr.

"Yes, I am a lab technician for Dr. Orr," Dr. Chan said, and bowed again.

"Do you know when he will return?"

"Uh, I don't think he will be coming back to the poster." Chan sounded hesitant.

"What do you mean?" John was confused. He looked down at his phone at the text message Satchinanda had sent early this morning: "Meet Orr at the poster session this morning. He will be expecting you. Good luck!"

"Where can I find him? Is he talking with another scientist? I have a very important meeting with him scheduled today. Now." Mend's words increased in volume as his patience wore thin. He was angry that he'd spent this time and money to come halfway around the globe to meet a man who was not there. He wondered if it was even wise to possibly trust such an unreliable person as the savior of his company. Satchinanda had told him that Orr was one of those fellows who had an answer to a scientific question before the last word of the inquiry was finished.

"Uh…he…uh…went to a place called the Simple Tryst," Chan said sheepishly and began to turn red.

"Where is that?"

Chan just shrugged his shoulders.

Frustrated with Chan, John turned away and wandered toward the main entrance. The late-morning light shone through the glass doors. He looked at his phone to get information and directions for this place, but the convention Wi-Fi had blocked the ability to view the website. A large, arched desk was labeled in silver block letters: "*Informatie*/Information."

John walked up to a very tall man in a blue blazer with a silver name tag that said "Franz." "Excuse me. Can you help me find someplace?"

"Ah, sure, it would be my pleasure. Where is it you would like to go?"

"I need to meet someone at the Simple Tryst."

Franz the concierge tightened his facial muscles awkwardly. He was surprised at the guest's frankness. "Sure. Need to let loose with this busy convention?"

"What do you mean?"

A very attractive brunette with a pointy nose standing next to Franz behind the counter smirked.

Franz hesitated. "It is how you would say…a sex show."

John's blood began to boil. He had to corner him there or somewhere near there, as there was a distinct possibility Orr could be dragging him all over the city. John was a very religious man and a dedicated husband, and he did not like the idea that he would have to enter such an establishment. Time was of the essence, and he needed to get on with finding Orr. He asked the concierge to point him in the right direction.

"You make uh…I believe…a left out the door. After passing over two bridges, you will make a right, and it's a few blocks down." Franz had wavered a bit in description so as not to appear to be an expert in this place, especially with his female coworker within earshot. He had laid out a tourist map in front of John and penned a circle around the location.

John thanked the concierge and took the map. He opened one of the glass doors and looked at his phone again. He was on a commercial network now, outside of the convention center's porn-blocking web.

The website for Simple Tryst was difficult to find, since the spelling was Symple Tryst. Once he found the site, he looked at the show times. The most recent show was at 11:15 a.m., and it was 11:20 a.m. now. Each show was an hour long, and he thought if he cornered Orr there, he could talk business. John did not care if he was interrupting Orr's show, as Orr had missed his appointed meeting time.

The walk to the sex show was a pretty one. Colorful, single-geared bicycles floated past him. He walked over small pedestrian canal bridges and watched as tourists in low-roofed boats passed under with smiles. He passed skinny brick homes with very elaborate masonry crowns on the top of them. The quaintness was somewhat broken by the smell of garbage and frequent sightings of disheveled people on benches, who John assumed were addicts. He then made his appointed right turn and saw large windowed storefronts on both sides of the street with lingerie-clad women posing in various positions. Clustered in front of the windows were Asian tourists gawking and snapping photos with their smartphones. Some even had selfie sticks where they could take pics of themselves with a prostitute. John was disgusted by the display and the men who enjoyed the activity. He briefly thought of the horrible possibility of his daughter pursuing such a profession if he and his wife did not work every day to raise their children in the right manner.

Then, a few hundred feet from his destination, it struck him. He didn't know what Orr looked like. He wanted to text Satchinanda to send him a picture, but there was a six-hour time difference between Amsterdam and Indiana. He remembered Orr's university and looked him up on his phone. On the cobblestone street, he knew the visage of the man he was supposed to meet. Orr had pudgy cheeks and sandy-blond hair parted in the middle. John hoped this photo was relatively current and that he hadn't grown a beard. He walked to the show.

The Symple Tryst looked like an old movie theater. Above the kiosk, yellow lightbulbs surrounded a pie-shaped sign. On each side of the pie were black letters that read "Kyle & Tara 10 A 11:15 A." He went to the small windowed kiosk underneath the sign.

"One, please," John said.

"It is too late. The show has started. You will not get the whole experience," a bald man with a handlebar mustache said.

"I don't particularly care about the whole experience, but I need to see the rest of the show," John said sternly.

"We do not usually do this," the man went on.

John looked at his watch and lied to the man, saying that if he did not get into this show, he would miss his tour bus. He also told him that he had told all his friends back home that he was going to see a sex show in Amsterdam.

"It is still full price," the man said.

"OK," John said and handed him the required euros through a small semicircular opening in the window of the kiosk.

John took his ticket and handed it to someone who seemed to be a pimply faced teenager but was probably older, much as someone he would find taking his ticket in an Indiana movie theater. He was ushered into the sex-show theater. John was happy to see that the lights were on so that he could see the audience and find Orr. But they also could see him, so he tucked his chin to prevent being recognized and looked up to scan the room. The seats descended at an angle. John looked down the rows of seats. The theater was thinly populated, and the viewers, both men and women, were glued to the action on the stage. The room smelled of cigarette smoke.

At the time, "Tara," if that's who it was, was completely naked. She looked to be in her late thirties or early forties with tan skin and dark hair. She had wrinkles in the corners of her eyes. The stage was a dark wood and in the background were various two dimensional cutouts of various Netherlands monuments. Her loose breasts were moving up and down as she bobbed up and down on "Kyle." Kyle's face could not be seen, only the bottoms of his feet and his hairy legs. as his back was on the floor and head was pointed toward the back of the state. John began to get nauseated and felt the eggs and toast from breakfast start to rise up. He focused on the rows to find some relief.

In the middle of one of the middle rows was sitting a man who looked like Orr. He was not glued to the show but appeared to be playing solitaire on his phone. John was thankful no one else was sitting in his row. He crouched down so as not to disturb the other viewers. He took the seat next to the man, who continued to play solitaire on his phone as if nothing had happened.

Tara on stage began to moan.

John leaned over to the man's ear and asked, "Barry Orr?"

"I guess you found me." Orr never looked up but continued to arrange his virtual cards on his phone.

Chapter 7

Before he met Mend that day, Orr was his usual contemplative self. He was one of those restless geniuses who could never relax, as the ideas and memories constantly bombarded him. In the morning before the conference, he sat in the hotel café, drinking his fourth cup of black coffee. The dark liquid passed his lips that were surrounded by two-day-old blondish-gray stubble. He had decided to grow out his beard while he was in Amsterdam. His eyes were half closed with bags under them. It was the second night in Amsterdam for him.

The night before, he drank until he couldn't remember how he got home. The alcohol he used to forget the previous night, which he'd spent with two ladies of the night. He didn't know why he drank to forget about the experience. Getting caught was not a worry of his, as he retained loyalties to no one. He had no fear of disease either, as again no one would catch a disease from him. But then he thought of his mother, and he realized that it was his reason for drinking away the previous night. He pushed his chair on its back legs and smirked to himself. Tilting back and forth on the centimeter axis of his chair, he mulled over his coming about on this earth as told to him by his grandmother. Possibly he was thinking that God would knock him off his chair like Eli from the Old Testament.

➤

His mother was a thin woman with a slender figure, pale skin, and shocking red hair. Mary Orr's personality veered toward anxious and jumpy. Her eyes always darted back and forth, looking for some surprise or someone who would come after her. Barry started to think about details about his mother that his grandmother told him.

Her parents, Fred and Judy Orr, had wanted her to stay on the family farm until she found the right husband in town. Unfortunately, she had a sexually abusive brother whom she was determined to get far away from. Her parents didn't know about this at the time.

The promises of Chicago were so close to her parents' Indiana farm, and she was desperate to gain her freedom. She left one evening without any warning after posting a good-bye note to her parents on the refrigerator door. At the age of eighteen, she would hit all the nightclubs and watering holes. She wanted to blur the memory of the Orr farm. Her sleeping accommodations were with both male and female acquaintances she met at the bars. She didn't have a job or, for that matter, any skills. One of her friends had suggested she take a temp job at AgUSA. The company was supposed to be expanding into a world agricultural concern, and they were one of the employers in the late 1960s and early 1970s that were hungry for workers, even unskilled ones. After about a year there, she met one of their traveling agents. This man would go all over the country making business deals for AgUSA and would eventually make regular stops at her boss's office. This well-dressed salesman would flirt with her before and after going into her boss's office, and she would return Bob Mohr's advances. He was six feet tall, with high cheekbones and broad shoulders, and he looked to her to be so sturdy, a real protector from all the demons that made her anxious. She didn't mind that he was twenty years her senior.

The biggest roadblock to their relationship was Bob's wife. Mary did her best to tempt him away from her. Eventually she would have him stay at her house when he was in town for a meeting instead of staying at the corporate suite. For several months, she thought her efforts were working. His love for his wife had diminished, but he had a son in his Maryland home who drew him back. She did her best to persuade him with sex and food to leave his wife. Her desire to keep him led her to stop her birth control without telling him. Pregnant, she hoped to make him a new and improved home in Chicago, no longer an affair.

Bob stayed with her a few more times, making her feel good about herself. She was ignorant to his true feelings about their relationship as only a fling. She never heard him imply or infer that he was going to leave his wife in Maryland. Then one day, during her second trimester, without any warning, he left. She kept working at AgUSA to save up for her delivery and to see if Bob would come to see her boss. He never appeared. She called and wrote letters to his office in Maryland with no answer. She finally asked her boss, who was never privy to their relationship. He told her that Bob moved up the chain of command in Maryland, and he didn't need to report to Chicago anymore.

Mary started drinking in her second trimester, and when she delivered, she came to a local public hospital in a cab, drunk. The delivery went fine, and he was a normal baby. The hospital staff had separated him from her, as they were unsure what the drunkard would do with this child. The attending physician on her case was not sure what to do with Mary, other than to dry her out in an acute setting. He thought longer-term care might be needed in a mental hospital. She was experiencing delirium tremens from alcohol withdrawal and was hallucinating. As the staff gave her sedatives, other nurses were trying to figure out who to send baby Orr home with. They found out where she lived from the cabby who drove her to the hospital. From there, the landlord told the staff Mary's next of kin.

Judy Orr took a train right away to see her daughter and the new baby. Mary, who was completely delusional and incomprehensible, smelled of urine. Needless to say, Judy's visit to Mary's hospital room was short. A lump formed in her throat at the self-made state of her daughter, and she dreaded what sort of monster was produced from her loins. The nurse brought Mary's baby to her. She cried when she saw the little miracle. The nurse asked what the hospital should call him or put on his birth certificate. Judy could only think of one name, and that was Barry, the name of the son who had killed himself. This happened to be the same son who abused Mary, but Judy had no clue about this.

Grandma Judy took care of Barry as a baby at Mary's apartment until she was released from a local asylum. Grandpa never came to visit to see him as a baby because he was still angry about Mary leaving the farm and was now even angrier that she had a child out of wedlock, all the while drunk. Judy and Fred were not particularly religious folks, and went to the community Episcopal Church weekly more for the social event than anything. As their friends sold off their farms due to an ever-encroaching suburbia, there were fewer friends to socialize with, and the Orrs' church attendance would be erratic at best. They still clung to traditional Midwest values, if not overtly Christian ones, and Fred thought Mary completely abandoned that tradition. The farm was passed down through four generations of Orrs, and much of the living extended family lived either on the farm or close by. It had even survived foreclosure during the Depression.

⌕

Barry looked at his phone and plugged one end of an earbud into his left ear as he continued to reminisce in the coffee shop. The poster session was going to start soon, and he didn't want to stand there listening to people who didn't know his research ask inane questions. He turned on a Carpenters' tune to relax and continue thinking of the past. Grandma Judy told him much of the story of his infancy when he was a teenager to help him deal with his mother. He would spend a lot of time on the Orr farm, and he remembered the rolling crops of corn swaying in the breeze. He would run through the rows to clear his head. He would play with other farm children. In Chicago, the neighborhood his mother's row house was in became rougher every consecutive year that he lived there. When he was in school, he buried himself in books so as not to get beaten up. At home, he would also become laser focused just so he didn't get a tongue-lashing from his overdosing or drunk mother.

He remembered when he was in first grade bringing a frog into the house. The cement and brick that surrounded his home left little room for nature. He welled up with pride that he had captured something alien. His mother did not look at it very closely, as she was flipping through old *Pop Magazines* that she salvaged before the grocery store threw them out. She had been working at the store part time, as AgUSA had been cutting her hours.

"Yes, yes, that's nice," she said dismissively.

"No, you aren't looking at what I have," Barry said in his small voice.

"What?" She started to turn red. "You stupid little fuck. Get that disgusting thing out of here. You're as dumb as the uncle you're named after. It doesn't belong here. You're a little moron."

Little Barry's shoulders arched back, bracing for a slap of his mother's hand. The impact didn't come but his big blue eyes flooded anyway. He had seen his mother angry before but usually when he knew he had done something wrong or when he was unassumingly playing in her way on the floor. Doubly heartbreaking was that he felt so good about this living thing, and his mother was turning him away. He ran toward the front door, which his mother was pointing to. He rumbled down the steps, opened his hands, and set free the frog on the side yard. A few days later as he walked to school, he came upon the corpse of that same frog being picked over by a crow. He didn't care by then, and he was happy the frog was dead so that he was no longer tempted to pick it up and care for it.

Bob Mohr, his real father, did come to the house once. His memory was intermixed with a variety of "fathers," transient boyfriends of his mother's, many of whom he would only see once. Mohr was kind to him and even gave him a toy truck. Barry thought he must have been in second grade when Bob visited him. He stayed the night and then left, never to be seen again. The day after his father left, Mary was in one of her tirades, yelling and throwing pillows and bottles. Barry darted past the landlord in the hall, who was curious to see what was going on in the apartment because of the noise. He huddled in a little fort located in a playground nearby. He really did not want to see his father again if that was going to happen every time he left.

Barry kept seeing his grandparents, Fred and Judy, at the farm. When Fred had a stroke when Barry was sixteen, there was no leadership at the farm. A relative who Barry called his "uncle," but was not technically so, was next in line to run the farm, had no interest in toiling on the land. Eventually, loans on the farm could not be paid. His grandparents sold the farm to help pay for Fred's care at an assisted-living center.

Barry got his energy from his grandparent's farm, not from his grandparents themselves. He stopped seeing them, and during the last summers at home he would involve himself with work at a local fast food chain during the day and at night in various nerdy hobby clubs. He rarely made close friends though, as they may have wanted to come to his shanty apartment and therefore would have also seen his stoned mother. He graduated high school with no one in the stands to congratulate him. A month after graduation, he loaded a duffel bag full of clothes and small items and headed out to East Kansas A&M. Barry remembers his mother laid out on the couch, moaning something incomprehensible. She babbled about being abused by her brother, and she was sorry he was named after him. She was thin and a little jaundiced. He left her a note indicating where he was going but didn't leave an address or phone number. He never heard from her again.

In his junior year of college, he got a call from a Chicago hospital. "Your mother died from complications of liver failure," the person said.

"Thanks for letting me know," Barry said coldly and was about to hang up the phone.

"Wait—what arrangements should be made for the body?" the person on the other end said in earnest.

"Whatever you would do for a John Doe would be fine," he said and hung up the phone.

The Carpenters' song ended and so did his remembrances for the time being. He decided he would put his technician, Chan, in front of the poster and play hooky at a local sex show. If John Mend wanted him badly enough, he believed he would eventually find him there.

CHAPTER 8

"**W**e want people to know that we will not stand for genetic modification of our food supply," Jessica Freeman said, a cloud of condensation leaping from her mouth to the reporter standing beside her.

The reporter beside her was a forty-something man with perfectly shellacked hair that did not move with the slight breeze. He held a black microphone with the call letters WEGG in front of his chest. "So what is the problem with genetically modified foods?" the reporter asked, as though naïve to any controversy surrounding the grown products.

"It has been well established that there are links to genetically modified foods and cancer, diabetes, and autoimmune disorders. Frankly, these foods are killing us," Jessica said passionately.

"Why would any company want to harm their customers? What is the point of this?" the reporter asked.

"Hell no, GMO! Hell no, GMO!" the large crowd behind Jessica chanted. Signs throughout the crowd advocated more natural means of food production. Some read, "GMO kills!" Other signs showed corpses piled up from a foreign-government genocide saying, "You're next! GMO!" The people were marching and chanting in front of the Capitol building in a circular pattern. It was a beautiful, early fall day in Washington, with a light breeze and low humidity.

Jessica was front and center in the crowd, in front of a podium with a sign that said, "NOGMO.org" and below it in small letters, "Join the fight to save your life!"

Jessica blew one of her curls out of her eyes and said, "Corporate greed is the reason. The agricultural industry needs to sell the most seeds to the most farmers who are desperate to sell their crops. They have no choice because they compete to stay alive. The agricultural companies continue to improve their products. They make the perfect tomato and perfect ear of corn, just like the pictures in magazines. These vegetables are not natural, and they are killing the American people. We want the US government to stop sanctioning the poisoning of the American people. New legislation for identifying GMO foods and whether they are safe or not is being proposed. We want food the way nature has intended it."

"Well, there you have it, Kadeisha," the reporter said to an invisible anchor several miles away. The reporter twirled his index finger about his ear, indicating to the cameraman that they were done with the story, and he trotted away from Jessica.

Jessica continued speaking at the dais. "The NOGMO group is fighting for our survival, as we are being poisoned by corporations. The greed and blatant disregard for Americans' safety should be our top priority and should be reined in by our elected officials."

The protesters cheered in unison, "No more GMO!"

"My friends." She paused again to wait for the cheers to die down. "We need to point out to all the legislators who will vote for the Subsidizing Agriculture for Eating, or so-called SAFE Bill, number one-eight-six-one, that we will not be killed for the sake of corporate profits. We will not take this lying down, because we want to live," Jessica said, increasing volume with each sentence.

The crowd answered her words with a huge roar. "Yeah!"

"The SAFE Bill is not for our safety but for the safety of corporate profits. I want all of you to write to your congressmen and senators and tell them to vote no on this bill. I want you to keep up the energy that you have shown me now. And use that when you go home. If you need more information, go to our website at NOGMO.org. We have a petition going around that will get you on our mailing list as well. We have a wonderful group of speakers today, including next a congressman who is on our side, Mr. Robert Frick from Vermont. He will be letting us know about a new SAFE foods act that will eliminate GMOs from protection. Several vendors have come out here to support us and to demonstrate the value of GMO-free foods. We have farmers from Virginia, Maryland, and Delaware who sell no GMO vegetables or meats, and they are here to enlighten our taste buds. Now, please welcome Congressman Berg," she said and stepped back from the podium.

Congressman Frick walked past Jessica, smiled at her, and nodded.

"No more GMO! No more GMO! No more GMO!" The crowd's shouts were thunderous.

"Who here likes their food all natural?" Congressman Frick asked.

"We do!" Again, the crowd roared.

"So do I. I guess I came to the right place!"

The crowd continued to cheer.

"Thank you, Jessica and NOGMO.org, for allowing me to talk about a subject important to every American's health and well-being. Some in Congress would like to sell out your health to corporate interests. They do not care if you get cancer or diabetes. I would like to make a SAFE-foods act as well. One that helps some of the vendors here, and not only that, one that gets their products to some of the poorest Americans. Now let me tell you what I have planned." The congressman continued laying out his policy initiatives.

Jessica watched intently as he gave his speech. She tried to digest as much of the information he was giving out as she could in order to formulate policy initiatives for NOGMO. Hearing the speaker above the fanfare was difficult, so she recorded every word.

Daisy was doing a taste test of the non-GMO smorgasbord in front of her. She sampled very green bell peppers that had some brown spots. The vendor had just sliced the pepper, and its unique pungency filled the air around the stand. She liked the crisp texture of the vegetable. Next to the pepper stand was an organic beef vendor. She poked a cube of steak with a toothpick. There were no chewy parts, and the beef disintegrated like butter in her mouth.

"Melt-in-your-mouth good," a tall, bald man said to her. He was dressed in a light-blue suit.

"Yes." She smiled uncomfortably at him. She was unclear why this man was talking to her, and she hoped he was not trying to hit on her.

"Sometimes it's hard to believe that nature could come up with something this tasty. You really think that they are lying and somebody added something," he said to her, trying to continue the conversation.

"Well, it's not. Our organization has vetted these vendors fairly well. We do not believe that anyone is using any GMOs here. We would end up with quite a bit of egg on our face if we were to be promoting a GMO farm," she said.

"Why yes, it would. I presume GMO egg on your face," the man in the suit said to her, to get a laugh.

"I suppose," she said dryly, to end the inquisition. She wondered why he was still speaking to her. The man looked important with his very expensive suit. She thought to herself that he had to be after something. He was an attractive man, with his cleft chin and high cheekbones, and maybe she believed he was some bureaucrat on a lunch break hitting on her. In the end, she didn't particularly mind being hit on by a man so put together. At these rallies she was usually hit on by crunchy comic-con types who wore leather sandals and unkempt clothes. These so-called men reminded her of her juvenile ex-boyfriend Gilliam. They made her appreciate Jessica's strong-willed, intellectual personality even more.

"Well, we have a lot to go over, folks," said the bellowing voice of Dr. Ronica James of Eastern Alabama State University. Dr. James was an African American woman in her fifties with salt-and-pepper hair tied in a bun. She stood behind the podium in a regal purple suit and began to give her lecture on the genetic reasons non-GMO food is different than GMO food. She gave her lecture with the cadence of a church preacher. The tone of her lecture was pleasant to listen to, but her content lost most of the crowd, those who were not whizzes at biology or could not follow a science talk without the aid of PowerPoint slides.

The tall man in the blue suit stood next to Daisy, who seemed to be listening to Dr. James and trying to avoid him. "Dr. James is a great speaker. Do you have an interest in the genetics of GMO foods?"

"A little. I'm more involved with the fund-raising aspects of NOGMO, but I know some basics. How about yourself?" Daisy was surprised at this fellow's persistence despite her continued terse answers. Eventually she wanted to know his angle.

"Yes, absolutely. I'm in an industry that needs to stay on top of agricultural technology."

"Well, don't keep me in suspense. What is it that you do?"

"I'm with a very large agricultural firm."

"So a GMO company?"

"Not exactly."

Daisy was puzzled. All she ever knew from Jessica was that all the major agricultural firms wanted GMO foods to save on costs and make more profits. "Who are you, then? Who do you work for?"

"Eric Feinberg, and I work for AgWorld," he said calmly, a big smile on his face.

Daisy's heart began to race. She was talking to the enemy. His name was vaguely familiar to her from a conversation with Jessica. She looked around to see if anyone had been looking at them talking to each other. Everyone around them, however, was clapping. She didn't know if she should run away from him. Instead, she stood her ground, as this was her house, or at least her rally.

"Much of my work could not be complete without the help of Dr. Juliann Wong of the Tennessee Technical Institute." Dr. James wrapped up her speech. More clapping ensued.

"So did you seek me out?" she said.

"No, not at all. Just came to learn and move AgWorld in the right direction." Eric nodded his head and smiled. He looked down at the grass with his hands in his pockets, kicking the muddy grass with his expensive black Oxfords like a bashful suitor.

"I guess there is a little break. Why don't you come meet my par—" Daisy stopped before fully saying *partner*. She didn't know why. She cleared her throat. "I mean, the primary driving force behind NOGMO."

"Oh, I do have a meeting to attend on the Hill. I would like to give generously to your organization, as I believe that AgWorld and NOGMO can find synergistic ways to get good natural foods out to people without so much scientific manipulation." Eric smiled the entire time.

"Possibly. I need to run…" Again she stopped without finishing, without saying that she needed to run this past Jessica. "Yes, I mean, I think running some numbers together to find a strategy to get rid of GMOs would be a great idea."

"Wonderful. I'll give you my card." Eric reached into his inside jacket pocket and handed it to her. "You know, we don't have to just talk business. Boring genetics don't usually keep me interested."

Daisy put his card in one of her jacket pockets. "Sure, I'll get in touch with you." She shook his hand. It was a firm, manly handshake as if he was a manual laborer, strengthening them regularly.

"That will be nice. But who will be calling me?" Eric asked playfully.

"Huh?" Daisy was clueless.

"Your name?"

"Daisy Montblanc."

"Sounds regal. It was nice to meet you, Miss Montblanc. Look forward to talking to you soon," Eric said, looking directly at her eyes. He walked past the vendor tents to the Capitol building.

Daisy looked down at the card he gave her: "Eric Feinberg, CEO, AgWorld, Incorporated." In the corner of the card was a red circle with the shadow of three green ears of corn in the middle. Her heart sunk for a moment. She didn't know if she'd had her first conversation with the devil. Mr. Feinberg seemed at least superficially understanding. She didn't know why someone of his stature would be coming to an event for the common man. He seemed also to have genuine interest in their cause.

Funding for NOGMO had been dropping steadily. Despite being nonprofit, there were so many expenses between facility upkeep, staffing, advertising, and preparing for events such as this one, a sizeable cash flow. Although NOGMO had small donors, much of the organization's income came from three or four large donors. In the recent stock market downturn, many of their top donors had cut back on donations. This year, Daisy and Jessica nearly had to sell their million-dollar home, as they could barely make the mortgage payments.

⨟

Jessica took her focus away from Dr. James's talk. She looked past the crowds toward the vending stand and saw Daisy getting a card from an attractive man in an expensive blue suit. Daisy had a big smile on her face and was flirting around seemingly playfully in her jacket and skirt. Jessica's blood began to boil. She didn't know what Daisy was doing. Making a deal for a big donation? Getting a new vendor on board? Discussing who-knows-what topics with a lobbyist? Jessica paused in her mind for a second and had an internal chuckle. Could she be getting a date? This bit of humor subsided quickly. Jessica's usually controlling nature took over, and the temperature inside her rose again. She thought Daisy was making decisions about NOGMO behind her back.

Despite Jessica and Daisy starting the organization together, she had always thought of herself as the primary person running the organization and occasionally ran new ideas by her partner. Plans would go forth with or without Daisy's say-so. Daisy herself would think of new plans for the organization, but they were only implemented with Jessica's approval. Jessica texted Daisy from behind the speaker's podium. She received no reply and did not see Daisy look at her phone. She watched as Daisy looked at a business card the man had given her. From Jessica's perspective, Daisy seemed to follow the man with a certain longing as he left her.

Jessica quickly made her move toward Daisy during a transition between presenters. She decided not to confront Daisy directly about the man. It was important to test her loyalty as a personal and business partner. "So how do you think the protest is going?" she asked Daisy nonchalantly.

"The vendors seem appropriate. I think the speakers are decent," Daisy said somewhat cautiously. Jessica usually didn't come up to her during a conference, since she was often too busy troubleshooting. They usually celebrated afterward with the other organizers at some kind of completion banquet. The conversation at the party would be a rundown of the good and bad aspects of the rally, and the organizers would laugh at the near rally-ending screw-ups that could have occurred.

"Did you talk to anyone or get a feel for how things were going with the audience?"

"Some of the vendors seemed to be getting some good sales, and why not? The food was pretty tasty." Daisy smiled at her.

"I could have sworn I saw what looked like a lobbyist trolling around here."

"I wonder what they would be lobbying for. I think I saw a guy in a suit wandering around the stands. I think he was looking for lunch."

Jessica was anticipating that Daisy would come clean with her inquisition. The audience began to applaud the final speaker. She had to get up to the podium and wrap up the protest. She grabbed Daisy hard by the shoulders, in a way trying to squeeze an answer out of her, and planted a wet kiss on her cheek. She said, close to Daisy's ear, "See you at home. I have to do some housekeeping with donors. We won't be doing any after party tonight."

"OK, love, we'll see you at home," Daisy said after Jessica let go of her. She smiled awkwardly at Jessica and waved at her.

Jessica was disappointed Daisy did not tell her more about the man she had seen her with earlier. She looked back for a brief second, hoping Daisy was tailing her and about to confess. Instead, she saw her with her hands in her pockets, strolling toward the Metro station without any concern for her distress.

CHAPTER 9

"**So you need** some assistance with your corn production?" Barry said to John. The room was low lit, with heavy, dense smoke throughout. The two were tucked into a corner table. The wooden, three-legged table was small and would barely hold one dish of food. John had asked Barry for a more suitable place than Symple Tryst to discuss his science and how he could help Quality Seed. Barry had talked John into walking several blocks away from the sex show to a coffee shop. The smell was unbearable to John. He scrunched his nose as the stench permeated his sinuses. The smoke made his lachrymal glands hyperfunction and start tearing.

A fair-skinned woman with dark, short-cropped hair walked up to their table and interrupted the barely beginning conversation and with a mixed Dutch and Southern US accent said, "How are you, fellas? We have a nice selection tonight. I'll leave you two with our menus, and if you have any questions, let me know."

John raised his hand as if he were in school and asked her, "Do you have a more ventilated table?"

"What? You're funny. People come in here because we don't have very good ventilation. It's like they're getting two for one. One free high just by sitting in here," she said, chuckling the entire time. She turned her back to them and walked away.

John looked at the menu and saw a bunch of different blended marijuana cigarettes and joints. The only food was mixed in with marijuana. "Couldn't we have this meeting somewhere else?" he asked, irritated.

"What do you mean? I brought us here to lighten things up before we make any deals," Barry said.

"You missed an appointment with me at your poster. You made me meet you at a sex show," John said, an angry expression on his face.

"Which we didn't get to finish seeing," Barry said humorously.

"And now you want to discuss work at a 'coffee house.' I don't care if Satchinanda thinks you are the second coming of Christ who will save Quality Seed. I believe that our dealings are done." John put his hands on the tiny table between them, which began to wobble.

The waitress came back with a beer and brownie for Barry. "Have you changed your mind about having something?" she asked John and smiled.

"You can say I have changed my mind." John continued his ascent from his chair.

Barry put his hand on John's forearm. "Don't blame Satch. I'm sure he warned you of my proclivities. Listen, you can walk away after I tell you how I can help you and Satch. But you came all the way from Indiana for something. Are you going to tell the board to go beg AgWorld for a takeover? Do you want those greedy dimwits dissolving the company your father worked so hard to create? The company you took over from him can't compete with the global conglomerate that is AgWorld. C'mon, have a coffee, no cannabis, and if you don't like what I have to say or if you don't want me at your company, you and Satch can try replicating my theories." Barry let go of John's forearm with his closing statement.

John slowly sat back down. "Plain coffee, black, would be fine."

"Coming right up." The waitress walked away.

"So let's get down to business." Barry pulled out a small notebook from his inside jacket pocket. He opened it to a set of drawings with multiple side notes. "Do you understand much about the science of genetics?"

"I know some science. Usually Satchinanda has to take me through the basics and then get me to the advanced topics. He does it fairly well in plain English. I do have to pass scientific information on to the board many times. Primarily, you know, I'm on the economics, management, and political end of running the company."

"Well, for all those things, you will need to know at least some of the genetic process that I will be explaining. It starts with this little guy over here." Barry pointed to a drawing of a wormlike object enclosed by walls made of small, equally sized balls. "This is a maize dwarf mosaic virus, or MDMV. It infects most kinds of corn and is spread from plant to plant via aphids."

"Satchinanda has told me he has a team hybridizing different strains to get a corn resistant to this bug." John admitted to some knowledge of the process.

"Now imagine that, instead of preventing the virus from infecting the corn, you try to get the corn infected with the virus."

"Why would you want to do that?"

"In order to get genetic information into the corn cells so that they make appropriate modifications to the plants."

"What are these modifications?"

"They will transfer information via the RNA. Ribonucleic acid is the blueprint for proteins. MDMV is an RNA virus that introduces it into the corn plant." He pointed to the drawing. "There is another protein here that increases corn-starch production. These two proteins enhance growth of ears of corn and the number of ears per plant. I have been doing this research in parallel to my rice research."

"Why are we doing it this way? Why not inject the genes directly, as AgWorld does?"

Barry took a bite out of his brownie, swilled his beer, and sat back in his chair. "This is where science and politics come together."

"Oh? What do you mean?" John took a big whiff of the air around him.

"Well, MDMV is a naturally occurring organism. Couldn't this be considered organic or natural? We are redefining terms. Governments and organizations define GMO as manipulation of genes in a certain way that would not be consistent with nature. What is MDMV? It is a naturally occurring virus of corn. What plant do we plan on infecting with this? Corn. Its natural host. No artificial gene guns or biologically naïve organisms that would affect the corn."

"So it's GMO without being GMO?"

"Essentially."

"How do we get the genes in the virus?"

"Well, that is the same as any genetic modification. We have the virus infect a corn culture—that's a bunch of corn cells in a petri dish. These cells have the desired genes. We can pulverize them in with a gene gun. Then this virus infects the cell, and when a new virus is made, viola! We have the virus that holds the gene that we want expressed."

"But isn't that adding another step in regard to making a GMO food?"

"In theory, yes. But what we are doing is mimicking a natural process of infection. How the genetic material gets in the virus should be immaterial to all regulations. No one cares about GMO viruses."

"Well, then what prevents all corn crops from getting infected with this virus? I will not have any kind of advantage if everyone's crops get infected and then their crops get bigger and tastier because they are next to a farmer who has my patented virus."

"Not necessarily. I have designed a virus that necessitates a key to unlock the host plant. So seedlings and young plants need to be exposed to a precise chemical composition to allow the virus to infect them. The chemicals make the *virions* stickier to the plant surface."

"And this works?"

"Yes, it has been shown in my rice research."

"Why aren't you working on the rice research? Why would you even consider working for me?"

"Unfortunately, I have collaborators who are already selling out some of my ideas to foreign companies in India and China. I never patented them, so I can never make any profit. The corn technology I have is patent pending."

"Hmm, well." John sat back in his chair. "Why me? I'm sure AgWorld would pay you a lot more money than I can."

"I don't know if Satch told you, but I used to work for them when I was a postdoctoral fellow. They are a very political organization, and the way these big, bloated bureaucracies work is by knowing the right people and kissing whoever's ass needs kissing. I wanted to try new things like this corn and rice virus project, but they didn't like my ideas and didn't think I was smart enough to make the results reality. In time, I was relegated to being a glorified dishwasher. The lack of confidence from AgWorld set my career back three or four years. I had told Satch that they would grind him down also. I told him to look at a smaller company where he would have more autonomy, like Quality Seed."

"Well, thank you for recommending him. He has been a great scientist and a great asset for my company. He has been more interested in using natural hybridization techniques for human-consumption corn and more liberal genetic modifications for corn used in ethanol production. He asked me to seek you out to help bridge the gap and find a way to continue our promise of natural foods for consumption using a competitive, novel process. So what would be the terms of our agreement?" John asked, smiling.

"I would like five hundred thousand dollars in advance and at least two hundred thousand dollars a year salary, with five percent of gross sales that use my technology."

"That seems like generous compensation and the most we would have paid for a lead scientist," John said, somewhat alarmed.

"You will be getting an original technology that will take several years for others to catch up to."

"What about the consumers? Any danger to them?"

"Unless they are a stalk of corn, they are not going to get infected with MDMV," Barry said with confidence, but no one had tested his assurances. "Do we have a deal?" Barry stretched his hand out.

"Dr. Satchinanda will be in touch with you with my answer. I need to think about this." John smiled and grabbed his hand.

"I'm sure your board would like to know something soon," Barry said, holding onto John's hand for emphasis. Barry knew that since John followed him to these places that were anathema to his conscience, he was desperate.

"They always do." John pulled his hand away and stood up. "Please don't get up. I'll show myself out."

Barry stayed seated and watched as John left the bar. He downed the remainder of his beer and waited for the waitress to come by for a refill.

John walked out of the pot bar into the fresh air. He took out his phone and looked down. A newspaper blew around his ankle, and he shook it off. There was a text message from his wife: "Please call. We miss you."

He dialed his home number. "Hi, honey. I'm sorry I didn't call sooner. It's been kind of an adventure. I can't explain it all right now. I need to go to Savannah to see my brother."

"What about us, your nuclear family?" his wife asked.

"Honey, this is business, not a social call. I will call you when I get to the airport."

Chapter 10

The light shone through the drapes of the top-floor suite of The Executive Ambassador Hotel off K Street. A glint of sunshine reflected off the high-ball glass containing rum. The air in the suite was filled with the scent of mint air freshener. The sound of creaking wheels from the cleaning staff was heard beyond the entrance of the living room.

Daisy looked at the side table and saw the red neon numbers 8:41 on the black clock. She was barely awake and reached under the covers blindly for her underpants. She walked into the bathroom and turned on a blaring white light that reflected off all the shiny white marble and gold fixtures as if it was the bathroom behind St. Peter's gate. She relieved herself and stumbled back to the bed with half-closed eyes. She sat down with her legs on the side of the bed, only to hear a groan.

She looked to the side of the bed, very disoriented, and made out the distinct side of Eric Feldberg's face. The right side of his shiny head, his high cheekbones, and his sunken cheeks were all visible. Daisy's heart began to race. She mumbled to herself softly in a staccato panic, "No, no, no, no, no."

She didn't particularly know how she ended up there and felt the pang of nausea from having had too much to drink. Now that she was fully awake, the hangover caused her to have vertigo. She leapt off of the bed, with her legs haphazardly trying to catch her from falling with each step as she made her way to the living room of the suite. Using the doorjamb as her halfway resting point, she thrust herself onto the couch in the middle of the living room, where her handbag lay. The handbag was buzzing furiously. She opened up the bag and took out her phone, which listed several text messages and voice mails that she hadn't replied to between late last night and this morning. They were all from Jessica.

Daisy looked at the texts from the beginning of the night, as she didn't remember the night very well at all.

Jessica texted, "Where are you?"

Daisy texted, "Out with friends."

"Who?"

"People I met at the gym."

"When are you coming home?"

"Later tonight. Just having some drinks. I'll see you in the morning. I may be late."

"Do you want me to come out with you?"

"No need. You relax. I know you've got a lot planned for NOGMO the next few days."

That is where last night's texts ended. Then there was one this morning: "WHERE ARE YOU? YOU AREN'T HOME. I'M WORRIED. CALLING YOU AGAIN. IF I DO NOT HEAR FROM YOU SOON, CALLING COPS."

Daisy's heart raced again. She wondered if Jessica had already alerted the police. She texted her quickly, "Coming home soon."

Her fingers moved from the digital keypad to her voice mails.

"Hi, Daisy. I miss you. Please call me when you get this message," Jessica said softly in her first message.

"Hi, Daisy. I know I have been a bitch these last few weeks, but I have been trying really hard to raise money for the organization. Please come home soon," Jessica said, in a second message an hour later.

"It's five in the morning. You're not next to me. Please call. It's OK if you are going to stay out. I'm worried." Jessica's voice cracked a bit.

"I'm at work. I thought you were going to help me today with looking at fundraising numbers with Gerhart. I need you for this. I'm still worried. I'm going to call the police to look for you soon," Jessica said, a bit more commandingly in the next message.

While Daisy finished listening, a call came in from Jessica.

"Hello," Daisy said softly.

"Where are you? Are you OK? What's going on?" Jessica said, very loudly and excitedly.

Daisy's head pounded with each question she asked. "Things ran a little late with some girls from spin class," she whispered.

"Why are you whispering? Where are you?"

"I'm whispering because I'm hungover. I got a hotel because I couldn't trust myself with a cab or getting on the Metro, and I didn't want to wake you to come get me," she said softly.

"Do you want me to get you now?"

"I'll get a cab. I'll be at the office in an hour."

"I'll see you then. I guess. I love you…"

"Love you, too," Daisy said, but in the middle, she seemed to have been speaking into a dial tone.

Daisy put her phone down and guzzled two bottled waters. She felt less dizzy and stood up. She still had a throbbing headache. She walked over to the bed, where Eric was still sleeping. Under her pillow she found a mushed turndown mint, which she immediately unwrapped and shoved in her mouth. By her feet was her skirt, and she bent down to put that back on. A sensation on her back made her turn head immediately. It was Eric's hand.

"Are you leaving so soon? I thought we could sleep in." Eric smiled at her with his eyes half open.

"You made me do this," she said loudly. Her own yelling reverberated in her head.

"I don't think so. You were having a good ole time at the restaurant. You really know how to put the drinks down."

Daisy looked away from him and thought of the previous evening. She could see herself in the background of the mirror facing her at the bar. Eric was smiling. Several martini glasses were in front of her, and she was holding a cosmopolitan.

"How did I end up here then?" she asked.

"I was going to get you a cab to go back home, but you insisted on staying with me."

Daisy then remembered getting into bed with Eric. She didn't remember much after that. A tear of regret ran down her cheek. Her chin was planted on her chest, and she began to sniffle.

Eric's hand began to massage her back in a comforting way. "Don't worry. I won't tell the missus," he said, in an almost gleeful tone.

She pulled away his hand. "I really don't want to have anything to do with you."

"You did not seem to feel that way at dinner when I made you a proposition."

"What? To be your lover or girlfriend?" she asked, through congestion.

"No, I was going to give your organization five million dollars," Eric said.

"What?" Daisy's mind reeled. She thought of how much that would take the strain off NOGMO and how it would improve her relationship with Jessica. "Did I sleep with you for that?"

"I proposed the idea during our dinner. You made the decision to stay with me last night after I had suggested I call you a cab. I guess I was the fish who got away. You said something last night about how your dad would have liked me instead of some fellow named Gilliam. You also said you wished your father could see you with a guy like me. I would have to say it was odd." He smiled.

Daisy turned red. No one knew these feelings except possibly her grandmother. She couldn't believe the drinks she'd had last night could be some kind of truth serum. She redirected the conversation back to the money to get both their minds off the desires of last night. "So what about the donation? We stand diametrically opposed to your company. We can't take it."

"First of all, as I mentioned at our dinner, we are not in opposition. The market is shifting toward nongenetically modified foods. We could use NOGMO to give us some credibility in the marketplace. We may be trying to go nongenetically modified food for human-edible crops and genetically modified for industrial use," Eric said, using the similar model proposed by

Quality Seed to win Daisy over. Whether he was genuine in his sentiments was debatable.

"I don't think we can work with you."

"It wouldn't be *with* us. You would be our watchdog," Eric said, to ease her concerns.

Daisy shook her head, wondering how two organizations with completely different interests could work together. She took a few steps away from the bed and picked up her tan blouse and pulled it over her head. She started speaking before pulling her head through. "People will know we are getting bought off."

"I really should have made this meeting at a coffee shop in the morning." Eric chuckled to himself. "We give to Feed the World's People. They give to all sorts of organizations that promote nutrition, basic sustenance, and natural foods. AgWorld has a seat, if not a few seats, on the board. Feed the World's People gives you the money in installments, of course."

Daisy slipped her shoes on and vanished into the bathroom. She teased her thick hair in any possible direction that would make her look kempt. She didn't have a hat with her to do the job. "I'll have to think on it and ask Jessica," she said, walking to the living room.

"You don't want to make an executive decision, even though you supposedly both run NOGMO? When I met you at that rally, I couldn't believe I was speaking to the cofounder of one of the largest food-advocacy groups in the nation. You looked like a disinterested audience member."

"We are a team. She always asks me permission for things."

"And who is planning the budget for next year right now? Think about my offer."

"OK." She stormed out of the bedroom and grabbed her purse on the living-room couch. She'd grabbed the suite's front doorknob when Eric blurted out something.

"You can also call me if you need to remember the good old days." He smiled at her shadowy figure at the door.

Daisy shut the door firmly without slamming it.

Eric, who had been sitting upright in bed during their conversation, slammed the back of his head against the pillow and smiled at the ceiling. He was happy to make another human conquest and even happier that he was moving all his chess pieces in the right direction.

CHAPTER 11

John Mend walked out of his bed-and-breakfast hotel in Savannah, Georgia, looking to hail a cab. He looked around, facing the old cotton market. It had rained late the previous night, and the grooves of the brick crosswalk still had water. It was a busy weekday morning, and on the street, trucks intermingled with clueless tourist drivers who were looking for parking. After a few minutes of craning his neck in order to hail a cab, a green-and-white one stopped right in front of him. He got in the cab and told the cabbie to head to a small dock on Tybee Island. John endured the trip of multiple potholes in a vehicle that rattled and pounded him with every divot in the road. He watched the scene through his window as various strip malls mixed with old shacks that had lost their useful zoning. The hopping and rattling cab stopped, and he slid off the vinyl bench seat, paying the nonconversant cabbie his fare and tip.

John faced a downward-sloping hill and walkway that led to a wooden dock that branched out into smaller piers. His wrinkled light suit pants, white shirt, and brown Oxfords made him look out of place. He hadn't planned on stopping to see his brother, but after meeting Barry Orr, he had some decisions to make, and he anguished over them. He also wanted to get permission from a 10 percent shareholder of the company.

The wobbly wooden dock creaked as he approached his brother's boat. Most of the other boats were empty. He hoped his brother was on board his vessel, as he had called him when he reached Savannah to ask if he was around, and he'd given a vague yes. His brother frequently lost track of time and was sometimes hard to pin down regarding his schedule. John approached his ship.

The boat was white and twenty-eight feet long. On the back of the boat in black scripted letters was the name *El Individuo*. The ship bobbed up and down, and John put one of his brown Oxfords on the side of the boat closest to the edge of the dock. "Coming aboard, Captain," John said to a man in a dark-green canvas jacket, shorts, and Hooters baseball cap.

"You are the best-dressed fisherman around. You know we don't date the fish; we catch them and mostly eat them," the man said. He looked a lot like John, with a scruffy salt-and-pepper beard. He was somewhat huskier than John and had a small belly.

"Jorge, it is nice to see you, too," John said, and as Jorge stood, John leapt at him to give him a big hug.

"So it is a bit early for my biannual visit from you. Do you need my shares or something?"

"I need your advice, that's all."

"I need you to make the money, Juan. That's how I maintain my lifestyle. On Quality Seed dividends."

"You mean John."

"This is my ship. John Mend doesn't exist. Only Juan Mendosa on this ship. Let's go for a ride."

"Fine," John said flatly. He didn't like his brother taking away his self-ascribed moniker. The old argument about his name would have to be put on hold, as he desperately desired not only a scientific but a moral backing for hiring Barry Orr.

"Take off the rope," Jorge said to John.

John stepped off the boat and undid the rope from the cleats. He then hopped back on. Jorge Mendosa turned the key and started the engine. It gurgled at first, and then it let out a high-pitched whine as he pulled out of the slip.

The waves were choppy, and the boat would lift into the air only to slam back down. Jorge, who was at the wheel, did not seem to feel a thing. John, on the other hand, grabbed the side of the boat and gritted his teeth in anticipation of another hard landing between waves.

"You doing OK?" Jorge asked his brother and smiled.

"Yes, fine," John said, yelling back over the sound of the waves. He really wasn't fine, but he knew if he whined about the ride, he would get a good ribbing from his brother about being weak. His complaints would only make the trip to the fishing spot feel longer.

Eventually, after forty-five minutes, the boat came to a complete stop at Jorge's fishing area. The water was calming a bit. It was a partly cloudy day, and the sun darted in and out of the clouds.

Jorge got out of his captain's chair and started getting out poles and gear. In the midst of his preparation, he asked, "So really, besides fishing, why are you calling on me today, Juan?"

"There have been new developments at Quality Seed that I need to ask you about. And it is John; you know that." John replied with agitation again about his brother addressing him in his Spanish name. His father also did not accept his new name, as that was his label for him. But his brother abstained from his new name, as John believed it was older-brother razzing that came with him being lower in the pecking order.

"No John Mend on this boat—just Juan Mendosa. I'll keep Juan onboard; John can swim back home."

"Whatever," John said huffily. The teasing kept distracting him from a serious conversation. He wished he could have met his brother in a restaurant for a real conversation. His brother liked being on the move and never agreed to a formal strategy meeting about Quality Seed.

Jorge concentrated on tying his blue-and-white feather lure to his line. "So what's the big question? You're not taking my dividend away, are you? That ten-percent share in the company keeps me afloat. Ha!" Jorge chuckled at the irony of being "afloat."

"No, it's not that. Hey, do you need me to set out another line?" John asked.

"Yeah. Here, tie a lure onto this." Jorge gave him a rod and reel.

"Well, I've met a very interesting fellow. His name is Barry Orr, and he is an agricultural scientist from Western Kansas A&M. He wants to introduce genes into our corn from a virus." John tried to get the line through a hole in the lure.

"Gimmie that." Jorge snatched the lure and rod away from his brother. He proceeded to easily pass the line through the lure hole. "So you are going to can Satchinanda? It's a shame. I liked him, and he helped the company through some tough times. But if it's best for the company. I guess…"

"No, that's not it. Satchinanda is not going anywhere. He is going to supervise this guy and help with the growing of the plants. What I'm trying to ask you is about the science and the scientist."

Jorge gave him back the fishing rod. "Now see that ripple in the water? Looks like little tiny fish that the tuna like to eat. I don't know the man, and I don't have his résumé. How can I judge the scientist?" With two hands on the rod, he arched his arms to his side. "You let out the bail?" Jorge asked.

"What?"

"That loop on the reel. You have to flip it so that you can let out the line. C'mon now."

John looked at the reel and flipped the silver loop, allowing the rotating head to roll freely. He was embarrassed at how rusty he was at fishing, as the last time he had been out was a decade or more ago.

"Remember to hold the line with your right hand before you cast."

John took his advice, and with his right hand, he gripped the fishing line to the rod and moved his arms to his side. With a quick motion, he brought the rod forward but released the line too early. This caused the lure to fly high and not out and eventually land a few feet short of the tiny fish.

"Eh, short. Well, let's see if the tuna find it," Jorge said.

"Yeah, let's see. So this Barry guy has the data and knows his stuff. My problem is his personality." John diverted attention from his short cast and continued his staffing conversation.

"Is he a jerk or something? You need to evaluate whether his personality is worth any money you will be paying him and the benefit he will be to the company," Jorge said, and launched his lure perfectly into a school of tiny fish about ten feet from John's lure.

John watched as his brother's lure was perfectly placed. "He is a bit strange. He has his own unique way of doing things. He met me at a sex show in Amsterdam, and then when we actually talked about his project, it was in a pot coffeehouse."

Jorge deposited his reel in a holder on the side of the boat. He sat back in his captain's chair and turned toward John, who was still standing. "Wow. Sounds like my kind of guy. Maybe I should come back to work for the company."

John's heart began to flutter. "That would be great. I could really use your help. The stress of the board's demands has been grueling on me. Trying to keep up with AgWorld is nearly impossible; they have so many resources. Staying true to the natural ways of selling and breeding corn as Dad would want only compounds things."

"Whoa. Hold on. You just listed all the reasons why I never wanted to take the reins of the company. If this Barry Orr is tolerable, then see what he can do for the company. What? Is it the science that you are concerned with?" Jorge seemed to sense that there was something beyond Barry's personality that John was apprehensive about.

John sat back in the guest seat, disappointed with Jorge saying no to his request. "Yes, I am concerned. He says he uses a genetically modified natural virus that infects corn. I don't know how that squares with Dad's idea of breeding corn naturally for the best-tasting, highest-yield plant."

"Did you discuss this with Dad?"

"No. I know his answer. He will say no, and then he will say we should stop the GMO-fuel corn. Then what will the board say? 'Oust this relic as a chair,' or 'Let's look for a buyout.'"

"You could always do that, I assume. Take the pressure off yourself. I'm sure you would be getting a very nice golden parachute."

"It's not about the parachute. I think that it's as natural as it gets, what Orr has suggested. The virus occurs in nature. The genes in the virus just exaggerate the production of normal proteins in the corn. We get to do it right, and we get to keep the company. I think Dad would appreciate that more than technique," John said, with a definitive tone. He began to convince himself of the science and the mission of Quality Seed when he said this out loud.

"Well, then it seems reasonable to me. You have my go-ahead for this plan. That is, if you needed it." Jorge smiled.

"Thanks."

"Hey, what's that tugging on your line? I think you got something. Grab your rod, and start reeling it in!" Jorge said to John quickly.

John started reeling it in slowly so as to not let the fish get off his hook.

"Reel it in faster," Jorge said.

John still slowly reeled in the fish. The line loosened. It tightened again but went straight down from the tip of the reel into the water.

"Aww crap, the fish is under the boat. Juan, give me your rod and grab my rod, and reel it all the way in so we don't get tangled, and grab the net. Let's hope we don't lose it," Jorge said.

John handed Jorge his rod and went over to Jorge's and brought in his lure. He then went into one of the storage trunks and grabbed a large-mouth, silver-handled net.

Jorge struggled with the fish. He finally brought the line over to where his reel was and began to bring the tiring fish in. The shadow was visible in the water now, and John put the net under it and strained to haul it into the boat. The fish flopped about and struggled, gasping for air.

"Ah, a blackfin tuna. They taste good?" John asked.

"Better than no tuna at all." Jorge smiled and grabbed the fish. He took the hook out of its mouth. "Open the freezer," he said sharply to John.

John walked over to the freezer and opened the lid. The freezer was packed with ice cubes. Jorge held the two-foot floppy fish by its underside and mouth and threw it into freezer. The fish instantly stopped when it hit the ice. Jorge closed the lid.

"Time for a beer, bro," Jorge said to his brother and went to another cooler. He opened it and handed John a shiny silver can.

"Thanks, Jorge. So why aren't you sitting where I am right now? I wish many a day that you'd be the one taking the heat from the board. You at least had a good science background. I use Satchinanda as a crutch many times when I have to talk science with investors," John said, explaining his ambivalence toward his current position.

"I was completing my biochemistry major, and I found that I had a knack for this subject. The thing was, I did not like it. It was the same as being a small child in our house, you remember. We'd come home with good grades and get lots of love and affection for such a good performance. So I received that adoration in college, and I fed off that. I was also pursuing what I loved, as well. And this was painting. I was taking art classes, and I was not very good. But like a girl you are infatuated with who doesn't like you, I continued to pursue. Our father's continuous pestering me about my vision for Quality Seed did not make me want to become CEO more. I decided I wanted to be my own man and continue to paint."

"Don't you wish you had a family?"

"Eh, it is hard enough to make decisions for myself. You and Dad are family enough." Jorge smiled.

"Have you spoken to him lately?"

"We keep it short. I spoke to him last week and asked about his health."

"He still smarts from you not taking the CEO job, even after this many years," John said, ignoring what his father may have said about his health.

"Probably, maybe as much as the direction you have taken Quality Seed, Juan Mendosa, or John Mend." Jorge chuckled to himself.

"You're probably right." John sighed.

"We are our father's children. We want to be independent men. We want to control our situations so much. There will always be conflict among us. Maybe we should be proud of that unbroken bond?" Jorge asked.

"Uh huh," John said in agreement.

"Let's get back into town. I know a great place that will work wonders with the fish we caught."

Jorge edged the throttle and turned the boat around. They headed back toward the Tybee Island docks.

Chapter 12

"You have the correct DNA in the virus?" John asked Barry. Barry had been working at Quality Seed for the last six months. Meetings were conducted regularly with the scientific team, but John and the board were anxious for the new product to be released. At this point, the scientific team was getting close to a completed virus, and John was there to learn of the progress. Three of them were sitting in a cul-de-sac at the end of a hall with many laboratories. The walls were covered in large, cream-colored, glossy subway tiles. John and Dr. Satchinanda sat on a steel couch with bright-orange vinyl cushions. Barry sat across from them in another steel-framed chair with bright-yellow vinyl cushions. The room was lit by fluorescent bulbs, and the outside light of the day could barely get into the room through the high-mounted frosted glass.

"The team has been working on completing some of my theories and designs I had been working on prior to my employment here, and I'd have to say we're ready to throw it on some plants," Barry said. He pointed to a whiteboard in the room. The drawings were left over from a previous lab-team meeting.

The tube like virus was pictured at numerous points in the illustration on the board in purple marker. In red marker was a line marked "GP." The red line was in between various other lines.

"Thrown on the plants?" Dr. Satchinanda asked.

"Obviously not thrown, Satch. We need to prep the corn plants to accept the virus. Then we spray the virus on the shoots. By necessitating a preparation for the plants, only growers who have purchased the virus solution will be the ones who get the advantage of the crop yields. We get the exclusivity. Otherwise, the virus would be able to infect the next-door neighbor's farm, giving the same yield without purchasing our product," Barry explained.

"Do we know the formula for the preparation?" John asked, as he wanted to see that the investment in Barry was moving the project forward.

"I'm planning on using a solution that I developed at the university," Barry said.

"Dr. Satchinanda, here, will need the planned formula. He will take this to our fertilizer subsidiary and make this on a marketable scale. I'm hoping the chemicals necessary are not too expensive?"

"Not at all. They are just the right combinations of already common fertilizers that will essentially open the pores of the corn shoots," Barry said.

"Is the fertilizer safe for the growers and the people who will eat the corn? I don't want to be poisoning people to get a good yield on corn," Dr. Satchinanda said, with some concern.

"Satch, the fertilizer is just combinations of safe chemicals already in use," Barry said nonchalantly.

Dr. Satchinanda was distressed. When John had come to him in desperation to save the company, he thought Quality Seed needed to take risks to survive. Looking at Barry Orr's research, he thought it would be a reasonable risk. He believed Barry was only taking natural substances and making them better. Dr. Satchinanda thought they would still be natural, as the genes weren't integrated in the plants. The plants themselves were never genetically modified, only the viruses that would infect them. These viruses increased natural proteins in the plants to promote increased growth and increased flavor. He had completely missed the possibility that the plants would need to be prepped artificially. He had always known since he met him that Barry was unconventional, but he hadn't counted on how seemingly indiscriminate Barry would be. Despite Barry's unorthodoxy, Dr. Satchinanda believed he was still a results-oriented scientist. Still, Dr. Satchinanda thought there needed to be a check on the fertilizer.

"When you combine the two common household items of vinegar and bleach, you get toxic chlorine gas," Dr. Satchinanda said.

"I've used these solutions before on test farms, and I have never seen a bomb go off or chemical reaction in myself or any of my lab technicians," Barry said confidently.

"If Dr. Satchinanda can see the safety data on the fertilizer from your previous work, I think we should proceed," John said.

"If Barry is so confident, maybe he should be doing all this work," Dr. Satchinanda said. He was a little afraid of what might happen with the fertilizer.

"You can have him demonstrate a pilot batch, right, Barry? But I need you to work with the team handling the plants. Vivek, you are the expert in that. See how the fertilizer works with them. I need Barry to make sure his virus works," John said.

Barry nodded his amenability to doing a small sampling with Dr. Satchinanda to prove safety. Dr. Satchinanda said nothing.

John assumed the lack of response from Vivek meant agreement to participate. To shift attention from the political fight and understand the science more, he looked at the board in the room and asked, "What is this 'GP' written all over the place?"

"Well, that is short for growth protein, or if you would like, God's plenty," Barry smiled. "This GP is going to give your company the largest, tastiest kernels and do it most productively. This is the technology that will make Quality Seed a pioneer and the number one agricultural-supply company in the country."

"So how do we tell people this isn't a GMO product?" John asked. He had convinced himself on his brother's boat, but he was again having some doubts about persuading the greater public.

"The corn itself is not genetically modified. The corn is being confused by a protein introduced in the system. The genes of the corn itself have not been changed. I think, John, you need to use your salesmanship to get Congressman Jackson to allow this to be labelled as non-GMO," Dr. Satchinanda said in a brief moment of team cohesion.

"So I have worked on five prototypes that—" Barry started to say.

"Hello, I'm sorry to butt in," said a slender Asian woman with dark-framed glasses. She was wearing a tan blouse and black skirt, and draped over it was a bright-white lab coat.

"Oh, wonderful, Ellen. Thank you so much for coming. So how are you coming with Barry's virus cultures?" John asked.

"We are almost complete with getting the virus ready to be applied to the shoots," Ellen said confidently. She was leaning on the entryway to the meeting room casually. One foot was planted on the floor while her other toe pivoted on the floor tile.

"Diligent, bright, and in such a nice package as well," Barry said and then stood up and put his hand on the small of her back. He had been making advances on her since he had arrived several months ago. He usually did this when he was alone, and this was the first time he showed affection toward her in front of Dr. Satchinanda or John.

To Ellen, Barry's hand felt as if it was going through her back and strangling her intestines. She gritted her teeth and with her right hand pulled his hand away from her back. The other men in the room winced at Barry's awkward advance.

Dr. Satchinanda buried his face in his hand and nodded. Just a moment ago, he had thought this was the most sane and contemplative meeting he had ever attended with Barry.

"Ellen has been hired for her intellect, Barry. Let's focus on getting this project done," John said to Barry and looked at Ellen, hoping she appreciated his defense. "Well, with that, I think we should all get things done. I'm going to work on a pitch to the congressman. Vivek, I will e-mail you the draft. I will need you to see if my basic English version of the science makes sense." John got up from his chair and moved past Ellen and Barry.

"Sounds good to me." Dr. Satchinanda stood up and walked past the two scientists, as well as giving Barry an angry look. Barry smiled back. Ellen followed Dr. Satchinanda closely before Barry could say anything to her.

CHAPTER 13

A few days later in John's office, John and Dr. Satchinanda discussed the document they were going to give Congressman Jackson. John sat behind his executive desk, and Dr. Satchinanda sat across from him in a puffy, black leather chair. They were both flipping through the manuscript.

"I think that you have conveyed the science well. But I do believe we should discuss the safety and the lack of data we have." Dr. Satchinanda leaned forward in his chair.

"Satch, I say this on page twenty-three. Look about halfway down. It's the safety summary. 'The corn virus is naturally occurring. It has not been shown to be harmful to humans. The protein we intend to overexpress from the virus is not harmful to humans in nature, as it is also naturally expressed in corn genes. The fertilizer is a combination of products already on the market." John pointed to the text in his copy.

"What about the combination of all three? Don't you think they will have a problem with this?" Dr. Satchinanda asked.

"I have seen Congress and the FDA give a pass to all the frankenveggies coming out of AgWorld, and compared to those manipulations, this is as God made it." John sat back in his swivel chair.

"I expect you to eat this yourself," Dr. Satchinanda said bluntly and looked straight at him.

"Of course I will. I'm not going to run away from my own product. I want to be the first person to eat an ear of this—slathered with a lot of butter." John smiled at him.

"If you are satisfied, again, I think the explanation of the science is adequate. I'm unsure if that is all that is necessary to convince Congressman Jackson of this product's non-GMO status."

"You're probably right, Satch. Let me bring Melanie in from marketing. I have already given her a copy of this draft. Belle," John said, speaking into an intercom, "please get Melanie Fuchs from marketing in here to go over our document to Congress."

A few minutes passed, and Melanie walked into the office. She wore a bright floral blouse and black skirt that appeared difficult to close around her belly. Her cheeks were doused in too much rouge, and her curly blond locks passed over her right eye.

"Hi, Melanie. You remember Vivek Satchinanda?" John stood when she came in and smiled at her. Melanie and Vivek didn't usually mingle in the moderately sized corporate structure but may have interacted a few years back. Dr. Satchinanda also stood up and smiled.

"Yes, I do. Good to see you again." She shook his hand.

"Please, let's all sit. Melanie, what did you think about my essay?" John asked her.

"It's fine. I'm assuming that Dr. Satchinanda approved of the science. It's understandable and probably easy for Congressman Jackson's staff to come up with a rider to a bill that will exclude our corn from GMO labeling. But you know he is going to need more," she said, with a southern accent that needlessly prolonged the time it took to say Dr. Satchinanda's name.

"What else should I do?" John asked.

"Well, give him anything he wants," she said.

"Bribe him?"

"Let him tell you what he needs or what we can do to help us get this exemption. Do you want me to come with you?"

"No, that will not be necessary, but maybe we can practice how we go about 'addressing his concerns,'" John said, making air quotes with his fingers.

Dr. Satchinanda squirmed in his chair. He wished the process was straightforward and that the natural goodness of the Quality Seed corn would be easily visible to the congressman, which would avoid the political gymnastics. He chimed in to the discussion to make sure the document didn't stray too far from the science.

The three sat together for forty-five minutes to an hour, discussing how to summarize the report and how they would address Congressman Jackson's concerns. Melanie used a lot of advertising buzzwords, and Dr. Satchinanda brought her back to earth with the science. Suddenly a buzz from the intercom interrupted their near-finished conversation.

"Mr. Mend, Ellen Tan says she needs to meet with you in private right away," his secretary said.

"I think we've got what we need to get our corn added to the non-GMO list. Thank you all for meeting with me. I will have Belle schedule a meeting with the congressman hopefully in the next week or two." John stood up.

Melanie stood up and left the office, and Dr. Satchinanda followed close behind.

⅄

Ellen Tan flew into John's office past Melanie and Dr. Satchinanda and quickly closed the door. She sat down, and before John could say anything, she abruptly said, "I can't work with him anymore."

"Who? Barry?" John asked, hoping it wasn't him.

"Yes, of course. You saw him groping me at that meeting," she said intensely. Her eyebrows bent downward in an expression of worry.

"Maybe that was just a one-off. He is a fairly eccentric guy," John said with a smile.

"This has been going on since he has been here several months ago."

"Did you mention this to anyone before?" He looked straight into her eyes.

"No, I thought eventually he'd get the hint. Then the other day at the meeting, I wanted to explode. I can't work on this project anymore." Ellen put her head in her hands.

"But we need you. I can tell him to stop. We're nearly finished with the corn," John pleaded with her.

"What makes you think he would listen to you?" She peeked her head out of her hands with tears at the corners of her eyes.

John came around his desk, crouched beside her chair, and put one hand on her shoulder. "We will work it out. I will talk to him."

"I have had enough bargaining. I am a damn smart geneticist, and I don't need to be treated like this. Either he goes, or I go. And if I go, you won't like it, as I will be filing a very public sexual-harassment lawsuit against you, Quality Seed, and Barry," she said, raising her voice and talking right into John's face as her own turned bright red.

"But I can't..." John paused. He couldn't fire Barry, as he was the head of the corn project. He also wanted to keep Ellen around as well, as she not only knew the genetics and the care of the corn plants, but she also knew her way around the bureaucracy of Quality Seed. He believed it would take several more months than he could afford without her. "Maybe we can work this out."

"How?" she asked, drying her tears.

John stood up. "I can have you work directly under Dr. Satchinanda, putting the virus on the plants. In this way, you will no longer have to work with Barry in the lab. I can bring that guy from one of the other labs. I can't think of his name..."

"Nigel Ahmed?"

"Yeah, him."

"Ha! You know Nigel has a pretty big chip on his shoulder. Why exactly, I don't know. It may be that he was a bigger deal in his home country. I like the idea of Barry having a miserable time with him," she said, with a slight curl of the right edge of her mouth.

"So that should help—"

"But it's not enough." She stopped him from resolving the matter. "I have had to endure his pawing for the last few months. I deserve compensation for that."

John didn't know what else she wanted and started quoting her figures. "We'll double your salary."

"And a single payout upfront as well," she said.

"OK, how about five hundred thousand dollars?" He was hoping that such a large figure would impress her enough to walk away. He knew he still had a sizeable amount of discretionary research-and-development funds that he had not spent. The corn project could net Quality Seed at least half a billion dollars in profit for the small amount he would give to pay her off.

"Double it, and I will call off the attack dogs," she said and stood up with her hand held out in front of him.

John was stunned by her daring and was angry at Barry for putting him in this position. In the small scheme of things, it was a lot of money, but in the larger picture, it was a microscopic piece of the financial pie and cheaper than fighting a lawsuit and a public-relations nightmare. "Deal—but we will have to put it in writing." He firmly gripped her hand and grinned.

"That sounds fine." She managed a half smile.

"I'll tell Dr. Satchinanda you will be in his division starting tomorrow after we sign the paperwork," he said.

"I think I will take the rest of the day off. Let Barry know, please," she said.

John didn't like that she was in complete control at this moment. He had to be on his nicest behavior until she signed the paperwork. "I'll let him know. We'll see you tomorrow."

"Bye, now." Ellen turned and walked out his office.

John leaned on the edge of his desk and sighed. He hit the intercom. "A few things, Belle. I need you to call Murray Sachs to draw up a contract for me. Also, can you let Barry Orr know that Ellen Chan has left for the day and will no longer be working for him? Finally, tell Dr. Orr that he will need to call up Nigel Ahmed from the GMO lab to help him. Thanks."

Chapter 14

"That's an awful lot of money," Daisy said in the hallway lit by stained-glass from the front door. She was trying to be as discreet as possible. Jessica had hearing like an owl, and Daisy responded on the phone through her teeth.

"Who is that?" Jessica asked in a raised voice from the second floor. Jessica had become more suspicious of Daisy since she lost touch with her that one night when Daisy was with Eric. That incident had been a few months ago, but Daisy had become more distant from her at work and during the course of the day at home. Daisy seemed to try to make up for her detachment in bed, but still Jessica suspected Daisy was seeing someone else.

"Just some telemarketer trying to sell me on *America Americana Magazine*," Daisy said. She remembered this rag from her father's house.

"Ew, that's the stupid conservative rag. Don't even bargain with them. Just hang up," Jessica said loudly again from upstairs.

"Done! I'm going out for a smoke," Daisy said and turned off her phone.

Daisy opened the one-hundred-year-old door with elegant stained glass, featuring hummingbirds and grapes. She looked at her phone at the call log. She hit **redial** on the last phone call.

"That was very rude of you to hang up on me. Are you calling me back to apologize?" the voice on the other line asked.

"Listen, Eric, calling me randomly every week or so may not work out. I don't particularly want you calling me at all. It was a one-off. A mistake. I don't plan on seeing you ever again," she said. She pounded the pack of cigarettes she had to get one to come out and lit it.

"I know you and Jessica have had a hard time with NOGMO, and I wanted to help," Eric said, in the kindest of terms.

"Why call me? What do you want from me?" Daisy took a drag off her cigarette.

"I need a favor from NOGMO and the scientists you consult with."

"What kind of favor? We can't just call one of your frankenfruits good for people. We will not compromise with regard to this." She didn't know what cards she held in this conversation but acted like she had four aces.

"It's a new technology. No genes in the plants are rearranged. However, a gene in a virus introduced in a plant makes the plant work better." Eric spoke in a reassuring tone as if the small favor he wanted was really no big deal.

"What does NOGMO get for its approval of this technology?"

"All you and the scientists need to do is look over the way things are done, and we will be happy to give NOGMO five million dollars and whatever money your researchers need to pursue their own interests."

"That seems awfully generous," Daisy said. She thought of her and Jessica's own personal finances and their difficulty in paying their mortgage. The temptation to accept the money was great. "How can NOGMO put the seal of approval on an AgWorld product? We wouldn't have any legitimacy as an advocacy group for natural foods."

"You are funny." Eric giggled on the other end of the phone. "Money is so fungible. You have been getting money through a foundation from an oil company. A Dietrich Scopes has been giving to your organization for years. He's an oil magnate, and he likes corn to be grown naturally. This decreases the corn yield and makes fortifying his oil with corn based ethanol more expensive. The politicians do not like high gas prices, as they lose votes that way. They regulate as a percentage for less ethanol in gas. Thus, more oil in a gallon of gas, less corn based ethanol, and more money for him. Nobody knows this guy, but he is on your books. I know that, since we've played golf together. Same way for us; no one knows NOGMO would be getting money from AgWorld. The money would come from Feed the World's People Fund. I've mentioned before that FWPF has people from our company on its board. The goal of the FWPF is to help poor countries grow crops in inhospitable places. We give a lot of money to them, and they give it to scientists and anyone else we would like."

"What if I say no?" She mulled over in her brain that they had already been taking dirty money when it came to the "green movement."

"You can say no, but it does seem like your last few fund-raising campaigns have yielded very low returns."

"How do you know that?"

"I went on Charity Discoverer, and they look at your books. The site is supposed to help the public at large find out where best to put their charitable donations, and it's telling me to stay away from you guys." Eric chuckled again to himself.

"I should hang up on you right now." She started to raise her voice.

"How would you like to make your full mortgage payment? I have heard you may be having some personal financial issues. You and Jessica have a wonderful home."

Daisy at that moment realized that maybe her meeting Eric was not a trivial one-night stand, and currently their relationship was inescapable. She didn't answer.

"Daisy, I can tell you don't want Jessica to know about us."

"There is no us!" she yelled into the phone. She wanted to punch Eric in the face. She wanted to scream out loud. The gravity of her situation and the need for Eric's money kept her from exploding. "What do you need me to do?" she said, much more calmly.

"Thank you for doing this. I will text you with a file attached. Print out the file and send it to your accreditation scientists. I will forward you half the money promised before the approval letter. After I receive the approval letter, I will send over the second half of the money."

"What if our scientists do not want to sign off on this technology?"

"My thought is that due to NOGMO's desperate financial situation, these scientists are not consulting as much for you and not making as much money, and this is putting a strain on their personal and research funds. In the carrot-and-stick approach, I would start with the carrots. Then finish them off with the sticks. I find that works the best. And until the money gets into the NOGMO bank account, I would refrain from giving Jessica all the details."

"I guess I will look forward to your file then," Daisy said in a defeated tone.

"I will let you know soon." Eric hung up the phone.

Just then Daisy heard the latch from the front door open, and Jessica came out. She was wearing a long gray wool shawl.

"Hey, are you doing OK? You've been out here awhile and must have finished that whole pack of cigarettes by now," Jessica asked.

"No, not really," Daisy said, looking at the ground with a half smile.

"Can I have one?" Jessica asked. She never smoked unless she was extremely stressed or at a party. This time she wanted to share a moment with Daisy.

Daisy felt guilty and dirty after her conversation with Eric. She wanted to have no bonding with anyone. She handed Jessica the whole pack and headed back into the house without saying a word.

Jessica looked at Daisy's half-smoked cigarette on the ground. She stamped it out with her sneaker and crumpled the remaining pack in her hand. Jessica looked toward the house. Daisy had opened the door to the house and did not close it behind her.

She paused for a moment and remembered a trip they took to Western Virginia. They decided to tent camp as an adventure. Neither had done this without an expert. Once at their campsite, the two tried to put together a tent. The tent looked nothing like the package photo. They equally yelled at one another as they huddled in the discombobulated, makeshift abode, and rain began to bounce off the waterproof fabric. They slept in their own sleeping bags, silent and angry about the trip. Then Daisy started to laugh. It was contagious, and Jessica did as well. They laughed because they bickered like an old couple who were together forever and like previous generations of loving couples would stay together forever. As Jessica looked at that open door, she couldn't muster a laugh and didn't believe for a moment that Daisy would ever reciprocate.

CHAPTER 15

It was late afternoon, and the light wisp of the Caribbean ocean breeze rustled the white transparent drapes of the bedroom pergola. Dark slate tiles led up to the bed. The wooden bed had a large fluffy mattress. Eric Feldberg lay facing the ceiling with his eyes closed. Ellen Tan lay on top of him, completely naked under a white sheet. She laid her ear on his chest and heard his heart thumping in one ear and distant waves crashing against the rocks in the other ear. Turning her head so that her chin was on his chest, she blew on his face to wake him.

"Do we have to wake up?" he asked, but not drowsily, as if he were actually feigning sleep.

"Let's go for a stroll on the beach," Ellen Tan said.

"This was not supposed to be a romantic weekend," Eric said.

"Well, you made it so when we had our little brunch on your private plane and brought me to this lovely little bed perched high on a hill. It's like heaven on earth. It's like Vishnu and his wife Lakshmi lying on a cloud of snakes at the dawn of creation," Ellen said, her breath shaking the hairs of his chest.

Ellen had met Eric at Midway Airport before sunrise. She gave Eric a metal briefcase with corn samples as well as the instructions on how to make the MDM virus and the prep solution that made the corn plants amenable to infection. They celebrated their corporate espionage on board an AgWorld private jet with a brunch complete with caviar and Dom Pérignon mimosas. Eric had a habit of gross excess and wasting good champagne on such occasions. The plane landed on a small Caribbean island co-op owned by several large corporations. The island was used to wine and dine various companies' clients as well as members of Congress and heads of bureaus to influence laws. The two of them had drunk enough to remove inhibitions by noon, and they slept together on the bed on the craggy-mountain precipice.

"I'm sorry you had to deal with Barry Orr." Eric looked at her and stroked the back of her hair. He briefly empathized with her, but in the end his petting was like polishing a trophy. He came to this island with various clients and female escorts and, if needed, male escorts, to sweeten deals. He couldn't in clear conscience let the clients partake without partaking himself.

"I've dealt with worse. A catcall and a groping a day is doable for me," she said, trailing off at the end. She was afraid she would advertently let on to this business partner that she was abused by her father and brother as a teen.

"Again, sorry about that. You will be getting a big payday, though." Eric read her signal of tragedy and shifted the topic to something more positive.

"Enough about money. Let's do that stroll," she said and sat up on the edge of the bed. She curled the bright-white sheets around her.

Eric sat up in bed. "Need to get back to the office. I have tests on the corn samples cooking now to confirm the presence of the virus. It won't take too long. You'll get your money deposited afterward. Five million dollars, which is what we agreed upon."

"OK. Well, let's just keep it business for the rest of the trip. I'm going to get dressed." Ellen walked to a dressing partition with a sheet curled around her. Behind the curtain she asked, "Have you ever brought your wife here?"

Eric felt the dig from the comment she made. He sat up on the edge of the bed and grabbed his boxer briefs from the floor. "Before we were married," he said bluntly.

"Is this place yours?" Ellen said, still changing behind the room divider.

"No, the company's." Eric slipped on his pants and buckled his belt.

"Do the shareholders know about this?"

"It's part of our marketing budget and was bought in the nineteen fifties."

"Well, where is that scientist, then? I want to get back to the disgusting Midwest, hand in my resignation, and move to a gorgeous place like this for the rest of my life," Ellen said, resigned to the fact that she was not going to explore this place. She came out from behind the divider, fully dressed in a white blouse, black skirt, and heels.

Eric looked down a stone path that went from the pergola bedroom to a main stone cabin. A tall, thin man in a lab coat was walking toward the bedroom. Eric finished buttoning his shirt and said, "It looks like your ticket out of here is on its way."

"Well, Dr. Hermann, what news do you have for us?" Eric asked the man in the lab coat, once he reached them.

Dr. Hermann wore metal spectacles, and his gray-black hair was combed straight back. He smiled at Ellen and then said to Eric, "It does appear that we do have the virus, but…" He led Eric by the arm to a corner away from Ellen.

"What is it?" Eric asked.

Dr. Hermann pushed his glasses further onto his face. "The virus does seem to have some volatile properties, and I do not think—"

"Eric, I don't feel so well," Ellen said from the other corner of the room.

Eric and Dr. Hermann turned to see Ellen trying to reach for the room divider and collapsing. The two rushed to her side.

"Ellen, Ellen, are you OK?" Eric said and shook her.

"Huh, wha…?" Ellen's voice was a moan.

"Dr. Hermann, go get her some water," Eric said.

Dr. Hermann grabbed some water from a flask on the table in the room and brought it to her. They lifted her head and tried to pour the water in, but she made no effort to drink. Blood started to trickle out of her nose.

Dr. Hermann took a package of sterile gauze out his pocket, opened it, and dabbed the blood. "I have to get a sample of this."

"Go to the main house and get some of the crew to make a litter. We will take her to the hospital in Haiti in the yacht. I know some people there," Eric said.

Dr. Hermann ran down the path with the bloody gauze at arm's length.

"Ellen, is there anyone I should contact? Any next of kin?" Eric asked.

"No." Her voice was barely a whisper.

Eric had already known the answer. He was happy to have found Ellen. She was cast away by her family and broken spiritually by their abuse. She had a master's in molecular genetics and could not afford to get her PhD. She needed the work desperately due to mountains of student-loan debt. Eric said he would pay her student-loan debt if she was a corporate spy for him at Quality Seed. Quality Seed was happy to have her, since she was as smart as or smarter than many of the PhDs there and came at half the price. Delivering the corn from Quality Seed to AgWorld was her retirement plan.

⅄

The eighty-foot yacht pulled into a dock on the western-most tip of Haiti. It was twilight, and a light breeze whisked away the mosquitoes. On the shore, an old, beaten-up white-and-blue ambulance drove up to the dock. Eric helped the crew get Ellen into the ambulance. A balding white man with a dark mustache and in rolled-up shirt-sleeves came running down to meet the crew.

"Dr. Robert, she is not breathing that well," Eric said to the man.

Dr. Robert looked at her and put his ear to her nose and could feel the hot breath. By now, much of Ellen's face was smeared with the continuous blood coming from her nose.

"We should get her to the clinic right away," Dr. Robert said grimly. It was a very muggy evening, and sweat drenched his shirt. Viktor Robert was a pathologist by training and ran AgWorld's food-testing center in Haiti. This testing center was used for testing AgWorld's most cutting-edge GMO and fertilizer products. The poor population was more than ready to get small monetary rewards to eat the experimental foods. There was no regulation or oversight in a very bribable country. Best of all, AgWorld could run this operation as aid to Haitian people and claim it as a tax deduction in the United States.

Two black Haitian orderlies in very tidy, stark-white uniforms took possession of the makeshift litter from Eric and a yacht crewmember. They loaded Ellen into the ambulance. The orderlies got in the front, and Eric, Dr. Robert, and his assistant went in the back. Before they closed the door, they saw that Dr. Hermann, AgWorld's plant-virology expert, had followed the stretcher.

"Can I come along?" Dr. Hermann asked.

"Fine. Hurry up," Eric said, irritated.

Dr. Hermann climbed aboard. They closed the door, and the ambulance bounced along the broken pavement of the roadway. The ambulance lashed through overgrown vegetation in its way. The siren and lights were not on, as it was a desolate highway, and they were on their way to Dr. Robert's clinic, not the local hospital. The passengers felt each and every tussle. Ellen's body was still.

Dr. Robert checked her pulse. He bent down and again listened for a breath. With gloved hands, he looked in her mouth. "We will need to start CPR."

"Antoine, you grab the mask. I will do chest compressions," Dr. Robert said and moved up and down on her chest, using his clasped hands and stiffened elbows.

Antoine had placed a mask on Ellen and squeezed a bag attached to it. They didn't have Ellen on a cardiac monitor, as there was not a working one in the ambulance.

"Give me that epinephrine in the bin. We do not have a line in her. We will just have to give it to her intramuscularly," Dr. Robert said, out of breath. He took the epinephrine pen and unsheathed the needle. He then proceeded to jab her in the thigh.

"What did you say happened to her again?" Dr. Robert asked Eric.

"She passed out with blood coming from her nose," Eric said.

"Did she have any symptoms beforehand or any other medical problems that you know of?"

"She was fine beforehand. I have no clue what her medical history is."

Eric and Dr. Hermann watched the scene with dispassionate, dull eyes. The same resuscitation scenario with Dr. Robert, Antoine, and Ellen occurred three or four times. The ambulance finally stopped after about a twenty-minute ride.

Dr. Robert and Antoine stopped. Dr. Robert bent down and reassessed Ellen. He felt no breath and no pulse. "I think we have to say she is dead," Dr. Robert said and looked at Eric.

The orderlies in the front came to the back and opened the ambulance's back door.

"We should do an autopsy on her to find out why she died. Does she have anyone we can talk to about doing this?" asked Dr. Robert.

"Not that I am aware of. We are not in America, and I would just assume you do what you usually do with the test subjects around here," Eric said, annoyed.

"All right, then. You two gentlemen wait in the office while I perform the autopsy. You wouldn't like to see this," he said. He ordered Antoine and the two orderlies to move Ellen's body to the autopsy suite.

Eric and Dr. Hermann exited the ambulance and headed down a path that had a sign that said Office.

"Excuse me, Mr. Feinberg, what was the young lady's name?" Dr. Robert asked.

Eric turned around. "If you need to know, it was Ellen Tan." Then he continued down the path toward the office with Dr. Hermann.

⋏

Eric felt it was an eternity. He was nearly out of batteries on his phone. He was looking at messages and playing games until Dr. Robert came out with his report. Dr. Hermann entertained himself by reading old dusty medical texts that had been sitting in the waiting area. They both heard clanging and sawing sounds coming from the pathology suite, as if construction was going on in there. Eric's phone suddenly chirped a warning to indicate a low battery.

"Oh, come on," Eric said.

Just then, Dr. Robert walked in. Sweat poured from his forehead, and he wiped it with his shirt-sleeve. "I think we can say with some certainty that she died of a massive brain hemorrhage," he said.

"OK. Well, it has nothing to do with us, and we will be on our way. What a freakin' waste of time," Eric said, still irritated.

"What caused the hemorrhage, Doctor?" Dr. Hermann asked.

"It looks like some kind of virus when I looked at some of her blood vessels under the microscope. I can't say with one-hundred-percent certainty without more tests," Dr. Robert responded.

"What kind of virus?" Dr. Hermann probed.

"For this neck of the woods, it would be dengue fever, but it doesn't sound like she had any symptoms prior to this," Dr. Robert said and looked at Eric.

Eric shrugged.

"Could a corn virus do this?" Dr. Hermann asked.

"What? Hermann, it has been too long a day for you. MDMV infects corn, not people." Eric suddenly became more lively.

"It would be odd. But viruses are known to mutate and infect new species," Dr. Robert said.

"The reason I suggest this, Mr. Feinberg, is that we had a little incident at the lab. I did not get to explain this to you, as Miss Tan got ill. A cleaning-crew person ate one of the ears of corn that she brought to us. Within an hour, he came to us to say he had bloody diarrhea and that corn he ate was the only thing he ate all day."

"Well, I guess we'll have to change our business strategy here," Eric said.

"Business strategy, sir?" Dr. Hermann asked, completely puzzled.

"Thanks for letting me know, Hermann. Let's try making sure this is a side effect of eating the Quality Seed corn," Eric said.

"I will do that, sir."

"Mr. Feinberg, what would you like me to do with Miss Tan's body?" Dr. Robert asked.

"What do you usually do around here?"

"We cremate them," Dr. Robert said bluntly.

"Then do that," Eric said flatly. "And you, Hermann. I want you to clean up that island house. Meaning, I want no trace of Ellen Tan around. Got it?" Eric said forcefully.

"But I'm a scientist," Hermann said, whimpering.

"And you will not be for very long if you continue like this. I need to get back to Chicago. Let's go," he said to Dr. Hermann and began to walk out the door. Dr. Hermann sheepishly followed him.

CHAPTER 16

"Why are they fighting?" Vivek Satchinanda asked his wife. Vivek sat in the breakfast nook as his wife made dinner.

The twins were in the living room. The girls were oblivious to their parents as they struggled with a boy doll. Devi, the bigger of the twins, wrestled the doll from her smaller sister, Seeta.

"I think Russ should fight all the aliens!" Devi said loudly.

"I think Russ should be with Beth and have a tea party," Seeta said.

"Well, what if the aliens get them? He won't be ready."

"What if the aliens see them having a peaceful tea party? They might want to join them."

"Highly unlikely."

"How do you know? Did you see them eat people? Did they eat Spot the jumping dog?"

Frazzled by Seeta's line of questioning, Devi said, "They're aliens, and that's what aliens do." Devi tucked the Russ doll into her arm like a running back at a football game dodging defenders. The twelve-inch plastic figurine was a debonair, well-dressed man with perfect black hair.

Vivek took the doll from Devi. "If you cannot play nicely, none of you can have the doll."

"Russ needs to defeat the alien warriors." She pointed in the direction of various plush animals—an elephant, a giraffe, and a hippopotamus. All had glazed, oversized eyes and big smiles, unaware of the coming attack.

"Russ needs to come with me and have a tea party with Beth." Seeta tugged at her father's sleeve. On the other side of the room was a small table with a plastic tea set. There was one empty chair at the table, and across from it was a floppy-headed female doll with buttons for eyes and yarn for hair, wearing a polka-dot dress.

"Either you two find a way to compromise, or you will not be getting this doll back," Vivek said, chiding them.

"I'm going to tell Mom," Devi said to her father and stomped away.

"Go ahead. She will agree with me."

Seeta, who did not throw a tantrum, asked nicely, "Now that she is gone, can I have Russ?"

"Nice try. I'm going to put him on top of the fridge until you two find something else to do or you compromise." Vivek placed the doll on the fridge.

Seeta looked at him with droopy eyes and pouty lower lip.

From down the hall came what sounded like a herd of horses galloping toward Vivek and Seeta. It was Devi, dragging her mother down the hall. Devi was spinning her footsteps quickly as if she were a bull, pulling a weight too heavy for her on muddy ground.

"Oh, Vivek, I'm surprised you are home so early in the afternoon," Lakshmi Satchinanda said to her husband. She gave him a peck on his cheek.

"We have to talk about work," Vivek said in a low grumbling voice to his wife.

"What? You didn't get fired, did you? I know that John Mend did not like your cautious approach to things. Then he hired that boob Barry Orr. That disgusting excuse for a human being," Lakshmi said excitedly and was about to spew more vitriol when Devi stopped her. Lakshmi had seen the worry on her husband's face once Barry started working at Quality Seed, but he had never discussed problems with him.

"Hey, Mommy, what about my doll!" Devi shook Lakshmi's arm to the extent that it wiggled her mother's torso.

"Stop it! Both of you go outside. Mommy and Daddy need to talk about important things. The weather is nice. Go to the backyard, and play on the swings." Lakshmi said, barking at the twins.

"Aww," said the girls in a unified coo. They ran toward a sliding-glass door, opened it, and ran outside.

"I don't know if I can stay at Quality Seed much longer," Vivek said.

"Like I asked, is someone pushing you out? Sit." Lakshmi pulled a chair out for him at an oval wooden table in the dinette area. She sat down and waited for him.

"It's not who but what. It's that MDMV. I don't think the virus should be released, and it's just about ready to come to market. John needs to go through some easy-to-maneuver government hurdles, and we will be ready for launch."

"Do you think it can be made better? Is Barry lying to John?"

"No. I don't think it's safe."

"What makes you say that?"

"Some men in my division have gotten ill. They have been on and off work awhile. After this happened, I had our lab people wear protective clothing. I have not seen Ellen Tan, my second-in-command, for weeks. No one has been able to get a hold of her. I ended up taking on both of our responsibilities. Also, a farmer, who is one of the many who test our products, had bleeding of his intestines for no obvious reason. The man was taking no medicines, and before he was ill, he was 'as healthy as a horse,' he said."

"Did you try talking to John?"

"I did, but he is contending with the board that wants him to get earnings now. He has also been assured by Barry. John is very enamored with him. He likes the idea that the company will see the same results as GMO crops without being a GMO crop. He likes that this virus is a novel way to improve crops and is convinced that this is an all-natural alternative that poses no risks to people."

"How does he know this without testing?"

"He doesn't," Vivek said bluntly.

"Well, when he presents this to agencies, they will certainly ask him for more information on public safety, right?"

"I'm not sure of this. These government types seem all too manipulated by the businesses that they are supposed to keep in check." Vivek sighed.

"How about reporting this yourself?"

"I thought about this. I'm not sure anyone will listen."

"I think you should at least talk to the local paper," she said, putting a reassuring hand on Vivek's hand.

"OK," Vivek said sheepishly.

"Give John an ultimatum, and if he says no, leave. Then call the local paper."

Vivek felt bad about doing this. John had given him a chance to flourish at Quality Seed when he was merely an anonymous scientist at AgWorld. "He has given me so much at this company."

"You can always express that to him as well."

"You're right. I'm going to the prayer room."

Vivek got up from the chair and went to a small room by the garage. Various deities were there. He lit an oil wick in a tiny golden holder. He began to chant a few words and bow in prayer. The struggles of Arjuna came to mind from the Gita. Arjuna struggled with killing during war and the duty he had to God and his family. Vivek wondered if he let John do what he wanted, whether he would be doing his duty to him. At the same time, he would not be doing his duty to humanity. He focused on the ancient teachings of *ahimsa* and the idea of not doing harm to living individuals. Despite the gratitude he had for John, he came to the conclusion that the greatest harm to possibly all humanity would be the release of the MDMV mutant.

Chapter 17

On the wall behind John in the tan-colored Quality Seed research and development office were several old advertisements from his father's time as head of Quality Seed. One of them said, "Quality Seed—Grow Your Best!" The cartoon picture underneath showed out-of-proportion cornstalks and the blurred-out face of a man in a straw hat driving a little red Farmall tractor. Another wall displayed a poster that said, "Grow Quality! The Natural Quality Seed!" A photograph of a farmer with a leather hat and a large smile was hand seeding rows on his farm.

John had lit a cinnamon candle in his office that was piping the spicy fragrance throughout the office. He sat behind a large dark-mahogany desk and two large computer screens. One tracked markets and stock prices at Quality Seed, and the other was for internal business. He had a dark wooden pen holder in the middle of his desk with a silver plaque inscribed "Most Innovative Agricultural Company 2005, *Ag Engineering Magazine.*" He was staring at his proposal to Congress and was trying to make sure he was comfortable with the information that was in it.

"Doctors Satchinanda and Orr and Ms. Fuchs are here to see you," said his secretary briskly over the intercom.

"Please send them in," he said.

Vivek, Barry, and Melanie, in that order, shuffled in and sat in the chairs in front of John's desk.

"Well, I brought you all in today to make sure we are all on the same page regarding the final draft proposal to exclude the genetically altered MDMV from the list of GMO foods," John said.

"I think it looks pretty good. I'm wondering if we need to suggest any 'independent' scientists to Congressman Jackson to corroborate our findings," Barry said. He used air quotes when he said "independent." The idea he had was to find so-called independent scientists paid by Quality Seed who agreed with their findings. Barry leaned heavily on one arm of his chair when he spoke and looked at John through black-ringed, bloodshot eyes. Over the last few weeks, he had been working eighteen or more hours a day, making sure the corn they were about to introduce into the market was as efficient as possible.

"I don't think we should be deceptive. We should get the most independent scientists we can. Possibly we can get someone like NOGMO to vet our process. It is to the benefit of all humankind that we do this the right way," Vivek said. He was sitting upright in his chair, stroking his mustache with his right index finger. He looked a bit disheveled, as out of anxiety he had missed a button on his shirt, scrunching it in certain areas.

"Humankind? Satch, stop with the platitudes. The MDMV infects corn, not people, and I know for a fact that the rice version of this virus has been tested in Bangladesh," Barry said, irritated. If Vivek was adamant about these concerns, he should have let the group know earlier, instead of after nearly a year's worth of work.

"Then why have we not seen that data? You say these things, but it does not mean it's true. Even if it's true, where are the positive benefits of virus in rice?" Vivek asked.

"I can't tell you that. The people at Baumkraft who used my technology said it's safe, but they're working out the kinks for production," Barry said, starting to raise his voice. Baumkraft was a German agricultural company that had used the same technology in rice. They sold crops in many third-world nations, and they did not sell seed in the United States.

"All right, now. Let's stop this fighting. I believe Barry when he says it's safe. I don't know how helpful it is to get an organization that has no interest in the genetic modification of anything to judge the safety of our work. They wouldn't have liked the Native Americans hybridizing corn to get what we have now. Vivek, you were the one who brought Barry here. Now, after all this work, you want to stop it. I almost think you are trying to bankrupt the company. We have had good responses from marketers in various parts of the country. I have heard of no one complaining after these studies," John said.

"Surveys and taste tests in all parts of the country do not constitute a study of safety. I want to know why two men in my division got ill and why one of the test farmers got some kind of exotic hemorrhagic fever in Wisconsin, of all places. And where is Ellen? She was in charge of seeing how the corn sprouts took up the MDMV. Where is she?" Vivek asked, desperate for an explanation.

"I didn't want to say this in front of all of you, but due to Barry's indiscretions, I had to give her a large amount of money to prevent her from suing Quality Seed. I gave her a large chunk of money, which I'm assuming she is spending right now, and I expect her letter of resignation at any moment and a defection to AgWorld." John frowned at Barry.

Barry looked blankly at John as if he had done nothing wrong or hadn't heard his last sentence.

"I'm not a scientist, but maybe we should let the congressman look at the proposal and see which way to proceed regarding safety studies. He is supposed to look out for the American people. We probably don't want to be in a quagmire regarding release dates with NOGMO scientists," Melanie said, smiling to try to ease some of the tension.

"I agree. Vivek, the technology is so unique that the FDA probably won't know what to do with us. I don't know why some of the workers got ill or the farmer got ill. We can't assume the worst. Anyway, this was not what we came here for. I wanted to know if the proposal for exemption of the MDMV sounds technically appropriate and digestible for the nonscientific person," John said.

"Looks good to me, boss," Barry said and stroked his stubbly beard.

"Technically, it is fine. Again, we need specifics on how the virus affects our food on the whole and affects people and their health. What is present in the document looks scientifically correct," Vivek said, banging his fist on the armrest of the chair to emphasize his safety concerns.

"I read it, and although I read your promotional items all the time, I still think that this is very readable. I think the congressman and the agricultural committee will not have trouble understanding this. Our proposal puts the technology in a very good light," Melanie said.

"Great. In four days I have to meet with Congressman Jackson, and then we can start production and sales. Thank you all for coming by. I have to get to Chicago to meet with the board. They will be happy to hear this news," John said, without acknowledging Vivek's noisemaking.

John stood up, as well as Barry and Melanie, and they walked out of his office. John turned back to see Vivek sitting firmly in his chair.

"Listen, Vivek, I know your concerns about safety but—"

"Here, John." Vivek handed John an envelope.

"What's this?" John asked, completely unaware of what was in the letter.

"Thank you for the last few years. This is my letter of resignation. The letter lays out my reasons for leaving. I have already cleaned out my desk," Vivek said and put his hand out.

John shook Vivek's hand as a reflex. "What is this about? Barry usurping you? Is it about money?" John raised his voice.

"Just read the letter," Vivek said to him softly, got up from his chair, and walked to the door.

John followed Vivek to his door and leaned on the doorjamb. He tried to make sense of Vivek's sudden departure. "This isn't about money. You know you can't go back to those bastards at AgWorld. They will just be using you. You know that all the data and technology you learned here is proprietary. I will sue the pants off you and AgWorld if you use it," John said sharply. John knew Vivek's importance to the company over the last few years and was also afraid of him as a corporate spy.

Vivek, with his back to him, waved and walked out of the office.

John sat back down at his desk and opened the letter Vivek had given him.

Dear John,

You have given me more opportunities than I could imagine at Quality Seed, and I am thankful for my time here. I cannot stay here any longer, as I feel that Quality Seed is not looking out for their customers and may, in fact, be harming them. I would suggest with my departure that you plan a safety analysis of the MDMV corn in a very methodical manner. I feel very guilty about my participation in this project, and due to my belief in doing no harm to any individual, I will contact Congressman Jackson and express my concerns for independent review. The greater good would be to look out for the populace as a whole and not for Quality Seed alone. I hope this letter convinces you of the need for more safety studies. If you need me to help with safety analysis before introduction, I would be willing to do so. If you feel the need to talk for any reason but rehiring me within the current circumstances, please let me know. Your friendship will always be valued.

Regards,

Vivek

John thought about Vivek's letter, and he was saddened by the heartfelt resignation. Guilt came over him, as the last words he may have said to Vivek implied that he was leaving for a better contract.

"Mr. Mend, you are running behind. The board will be waiting for you," his secretary's voice squawked from the intercom.

John grabbed his coat and walked out of his office. He thanked his secretary for the reminder and proceeded out of the building. As soon as he sat in his car, he continued to dwell on Vivek's letter. He pulled out his cellphone and texted Barry, "I have second thoughts on doing a safety analysis."

He shoved the cell phone into his jacket pocket. The day was relatively mild for early March, and he thought about putting the top down on his convertible. In the end he believed it was prudent to eliminate distractions and think more about what he was going to say or possibly even give a dry run of his proposal to Congressman Jackson.

The blue convertible he drove dashed away from Quality Seed corporate headquarters down the winding driveway bordered by immature cornfields. He drove toward Highway 64 north toward Chicago, pondering his board meeting and trying to avoid traffic.

⬥

John walked through the revolving front door of the giant black-glass obelisk. Quality Seed leased a quarter of a floor in the middle of the tower. The only purpose was touchdown space for the board. They did not want to travel to Quality Seed's headquarters. If a board member was not from Chicago, they had plenty of hotels to stay at overnight. Chicago's two large airports made it easy for the board to get in and out quickly. The space was sterile, with gray and brown walls, and was practically empty. John walked down a hall to the corner conference room. On his way to the boardroom, he passed a glass wall and behind it, columns of gray cubicles, where workers fielded calls about orders and billing problems. A separate call center for technical assistance was still located at Quality Seed headquarters. John entered the conference room with a large oak table surrounded by high-back leather chairs. They were all empty except for one in the corner of the room. Seated there was a bald man with round glasses in a brown suit, looking at some papers in a folio.

"Oh hi, Roger. I think I was a little bit late. Where is the rest of the board?" John asked, puzzled by the lack of other members.

"They are not coming. I thought your secretary told you. It's just you and me today," Roger said calmly and closed the folio. Roger Ingersoll was the third-largest shareholder of Quality Seed. John and his brother held about 45 percent of shares and thus wielded considerable power but not absolute power regarding the direction of the company.

John swallowed. He didn't want to pick a fight with Roger, especially with the emotional day he had already experienced. "Roger, couldn't we have talked on the phone?"

Roger had a dark mustache, which he wiggled a bit before he answered. He walked toward John. He was a little more than five feet tall and looked up at him as he spoke. "John, I thought we should have this conversation in person. We need to talk about company growth. Specifically, share prices are stagnant. Please sit."

"Yes, well, you know we are coming out with a corn that will revolutionize productivity and taste," John said, taking his seat by Roger and his folio.

"That's great, wonderful, but the efficiency of the company as a whole will be dragging these innovations," Roger said. They then spent the next twenty or thirty minutes breaking down the company's finances by division and product line.

"So what is your plan?" John asked, hoping for an answer he would like.

"The plan is to spin off the divisions that are either not growing or, in fact, losing money," Roger said.

John thought about it for a minute. He had spent the last ten years building some of the divisions of Quality Seed internally or buying smaller companies. He had thought that each small division was integral to another's function. John also thought the acquisitions prevented a potential buyout of the company. "That would make us a smaller entity and possibly have us taken over," he said bluntly.

"Those things may happen. What I'm looking at from my standpoint is the share price for my fund. My shareholders come first. Legacy, tradition, and excesses are not in line with share price. What I want is a streamlined business that makes the most profit. If in doing so, someone else plans a hostile takeover of the remaining company, so be it, as long as we get a good price for those shares." Roger represented the Screwtape Fund. Nearly twenty years ago, he started a fund that bought Steeltown Screws, which manufactured fasteners in Pittsburgh, Pennsylvania, and Cleveland Adhesive, which manufactured tape in Cleveland, Ohio. Roger used the streamlining process to increase profits dramatically in the first two years, but eventually both businesses were sold to a Chinese company, and all the jobs in the United States related to those companies vanished.

"I don't think we should act too hastily. Let's wait until the MDMV-enhanced corn comes out. Within a quarter you will see that all the cogs in the wheel are 'streamlined,' as you say, without need for jettisoning them," John said. He was beginning to see his company slip away right before his eyes.

"Well, you better get that product out soon. My shareholders do not wish to keep waiting." Roger stood up and headed for the door. "Oh, one more thing. Don't bother calling the other board members. I tallied the votes already, and I have enough who are on the same page as me." He smiled and left the room.

John was beleaguered after losing Vivek and now possibly losing his company. He rubbed his brow at the table.

Buzz. Buzz. Buzz.

The annoying buzzing had been going on the entire time he was with Roger. John searched his jacket pocket and pulled out his cell phone. There were numerous messages from Barry.

"What?"

"We don't need to. It is completely safe, as I have mentioned before."

"Let me know what you had in mind."

"Don't decide until we talk."

"Where are you? I looked in your office, and you weren't there. No secretary, either."

"Call me, please."

John saw he also had several voice mails from Barry. In desperation, he knew he could not wait for any safety analysis. He was going to take his chances with Congressman Jackson, and if he requested a review of the technology, then he would face the consequences with Roger. Hopefully, the MDMV corn would work out beyond expectations, and he could convince a majority of board members to vote to keep the company whole.

He texted Barry with new resolve. "Sorry, in a meeting. No delays foreseeable. Will be moving forward. Talk to you tomorrow."

Chapter 18

John sat in the waiting area of Congressman Herbert Jackson's office. The sounds of the congressman's secretary typing away were audible. Occasionally while she was typing, she would speak to someone via her headset. The woman looked to be in her late fifties, with curly, grayish-black hair and oversized glasses. She sat at a large wooden desk with papers neatly piled on small racks. The waiting area was full of pictures of the congressman with dignitaries. There were pictures of him with various US presidents, civil-rights figures, and even an old faded picture of him with a grade-school football team from his district. He also had artifacts hanging on the wall, including a Native American peace pipe, a tribal walking stick from the president of Zimbabwe, and in a small hanging glass cabinet, a piece of the Berlin wall. John inspected all these items from his seat and considered using an "icebreaker" regarding these items before he delved into his proposal.

Just then, he saw Eric Feldberg rush into the office. He was wearing a light-gray suit and carrying a briefcase. He gave John a quick nod and a smile.

"Hey, Trish, congressman in?" Eric said to the secretary.

Trish moved the headset microphone from her mouth. "Yes, but he has other engagements."

"Oh well," Eric said and quickly opened the door to Congressman Jackson's office.

"Wait! Wait!" Trish said and stood up.

It was too late. Eric had closed the door behind himself.

John did not know what to think. Was he going to have to meet Congressman Jackson with Eric? Was Eric going to undermine him before he met with the congressman? He was beginning to think the deck was stacked against him just when he thought he could actually beat the biggest agricultural firms. He sighed a bit and started twitching his leg.

⋏

"Wow, she was all excited. You'd think you were having sex with an intern in here," Eric said. He put his briefcase down in one of the two chairs in front of the congressman's desk, and he sat in the other.

Congressman Jackson was on the phone, and he put his hand on the receiver after Eric's comment. "Excuse me. I'm on the phone with my wife."

He continued on the phone. "OK, dear. Yes, I'll...We can go to the new Caribbean place tonight. Bessell and his wife will join us." He paused. "Yes, I know they are wet blankets but...Anyway, I have to go. I have a constituent waiting for me. Bye." He put down the phone.

"Is that wife number four or seven?" Eric said flippantly.

"Three," Jackson said flatly. The seventy-year-old African American man leaned forward and wrinkled his brow. The light above gleamed off his bald head. "Have you ever heard of appointments?"

"Do we really need to fight? Should I remind you who got you this chairmanship?" Eric said calmly. Jackson was given the position of chairman of the Agricultural Committee after Eric influenced many of the congressmen to vote for him. The influence came in various forms of bribery and blackmail.

"I could have had another committee member in here. That would not look so good. I don't want us looking so cozy. Oh, and just wait a minute." Jackson held his finger up. "Trish, please let Mr. Mend know it will be a few minutes."

"Herb, the reason I'm here on short notice is John Mend," Eric said and crossed his legs.

"I figured that. So you want me to squash this MDMV enhanced corn? Apparently it may have some safety issues. I got a letter from one of his former top scientists, a Vivek Satch-i-something. Is this guy working for you now?"

"Satchinanda left him? Hmm, interesting. No, he is not working for me. Don't worry about the safety issues." Eric uncrossed his legs. He wondered about the implications on Quality Seed and potentially AgWorld of Satchinanda leaving. He reached down to his briefcase and took out a white binder. "Here," Eric said and tossed the binder in front of Congressman Jackson.

Jackson jumped back, thinking he would get hit. "What's this?" he asked, puzzled.

"These are statements by NOGMO-affiliated scientists vouching for the safety of the MDMV enhanced corn," Eric said confidently.

"Why do you want me to help Quality Seed?" Jackson raised his right eyebrow.

"You know me. I'm an aboveboard guy. I want a fair fight. Plus, I have some inside information that Roger Ingersoll is looking to divide the company. I'll let Quality Seed work out the kinks, and then we can take over when all the productivity bugs of the MDMV are worked out and Quality Seed has shrunk," Eric said with a poker face.

"Ingersoll, huh?" Jackson sat back in his chair and tented his fingers. "So what's in it for me if I approve this?"

"Well, what do you need?" Eric leaned forward with his elbows on his knees.

"I was looking to put a history-of-slavery museum downtown in my district. It would be nice if AgWorld could contribute to the materials. AgWorld would get a nice plaque and positive publicity." Jackson smiled.

Eric chuckled to himself. "You'd get a bigger plaque."

"That may be true. How do I present this to the other committee members?"

"Tell the positives from Mend's perspective and the NOGMO endorsement. Then let them know to buy AgWorld stock after the bill exempting the MDMV corn from regulation is passed. AgWorld stock will be the lowest it has been in a few years when people find out one of their biggest competitors has scooped them. Then, after the takeover of Quality Seed, our stock will be at its highest ever." This was not his intention at all. He had already seen that there were too many redundancies between Quality Seed and AgWorld, yielding few benefits. Quality Seed was also always a pesky rival who would pilfer business and scientists like Vivek Satchinanda from them. Eric wanted to see the utter implosion of his rival, but he knew Jackson would not agree to corporate vengeance, especially if any untoward effects of the MDMV corn could be detrimental to his congressional seat and position as head of the committee.

"That sounds like a good plan." Jackson rocked in his chair.

Eric stood up and closed his briefcase. He walked toward the door of the office and opened it. He turned back and said, "Well, it was nice talking to you, Congressman. Please let my office know how I can help you out."

Jackson waved to Eric. Eric closed the door behind him and smiled at John, who was sitting in the waiting area

"Hey, John Mend! How are you doing? You caught the congressman on a good day. We'll have to catch up one of these days. Have your office call mine." Eric reached out for John's hand and then with his other hand, covered John's.

"Fine. Yes, we should," John said, surprised at the greeting.

Eric left the waiting area as quickly as he had entered. As soon as he left the office, he took out his phone and texted Daisy, "Thanks for your help. The other half of the money will be sent to all involved. Do you want to grab some dinner?"

⋏

In Daisy and Jessica's home, Daisy's phone sat on their armoire, buzzing away while Daisy was taking a shower. Jessica, who was on her way out but had forgotten her house keys, heard the buzzing. She heard the water running and knew Daisy was in the shower. She picked up the phone and looked at the message. Jessica contemplated the meaning of the message for their relationship and the organization. She couldn't argue with Daisy or investigate more, as she was running late for a fund raiser. She put the down the phone and ran out of the house with pangs of anxiety in her stomach.

⋏

"Mr. Mend, I'm sorry that this has taken so long. Let me check if the congressman is ready for you," Trish said in a somewhat whiny tone, like an adult talking to a small child.

"Fine," John said and nodded.

A few minutes went by, and Trish piped up again. "Mr. Mend, Congressman Jackson is ready to see you now. You can head on in."

Congressman Jackson stood up from his chair and put his hand out. "Mr. Mend, pleasure to meet you, sir."

"Congressman Jackson, the pleasure is all mine." John shook his hand nervously.

"Please call me Herb. Have a seat." Jackson motioned to the chair.

"Thank you." John sat down. He looked around at the room, noting that the walls were less cluttered than in the waiting area. Behind the congressman was a window with white metal blinds drawn and framed with velvet drapes. Beside the drapes on one side was a certificate from the Alabama Bar Association. Underneath that was a picture of a very young Herb Jackson with Martin Luther King Jr. On the other side of the drapes were two certificates of graduation, one for undergraduate studies at Yale and the other a law degree. The walls on the side had bookshelves that held what looked like mostly legal texts.

"So as I understand it, you want the committee to green-light this—what do you call it—MDMV-enhanced corn," Jackson said.

"Yes, sir. I don't believe we fall into any category of modified foods," John said.

"I looked at your prospectus. I don't see a lot of safety data. And I have received a note from a former employee of yours who has some concerns." Jackson folded his hands on the table.

"Studies in rice have been performed as noted in the text. And I wouldn't worry about Dr. Satchinanda, if that is who wrote you. He is a disgruntled employee," John said.

"Well, he wanted us to run this by NOGMO. And we did." Jackson looked John dead in the eye.

John gulped, anticipating disappointment.

"And they concur with your statements. They say the MDMV-enhanced corn is safe." Jackson smiled.

John wanted to jump for joy right in the office but kept steady. "Well, I knew it all along." He smiled back.

"Here, pull up a chair. I am not a scientist. Can you explain to me how this all works? I have to explain this to my fellow committee members," Jackson said and pulled his chair out a little.

John picked up the chair he was sitting in and planted it next to Jackson. Together they went through how the MDMV virus worked. John explained how the virus was applied to plants. He also explained how taste tests had MDMV-enhanced corn beating out other varieties on the market. Charts and graphs he showed Jackson demonstrated that yield of the plants had increased as well. They talked for more than an hour.

Jackson sat back in his chair. "I don't think we even need a hearing. I think the rider to the new food-safety bill should pass seamlessly. My constituents may wonder how this benefits them, though."

"I guess it may help the nutrition of your constituents," John said.

"Ha! My constituents have eaten their fair share of cornbread, and more of them have diabetes than don't," Jackson said.

John started to get nervous and hesitatingly said, "I'm not sure what you are getting at."

"Well, you know as a minority business owner how difficult it is to get contracts."

Since he had been running Quality Seed, John had been trying to run away from the term *minority business owner*. This statement grated on him, and he had even changed his name to prove to others he could achieve success without identity politics. He didn't want to say something to lose his chances of the MDMV-enhanced corn not being exempted, but he wanted to clarify if he was getting special privileges. "You are not exempting the corn because of my minority status."

"No, no, no." Jackson shook his head. "This product is great on its own merit. What I'd like, however, is your help. My brother is a contractor, and I think if you could financially assist him in the labor portion of building a slavery-education museum in my district, my constituents would truly be grateful. And we would get you and your company a nice plaque for the support."

John was relieved and oblivious to the pay-to-play scenario Jackson gave him. "Sure, let me know how I can help."

"Let me write down the details. The hearing will be in another week or so, and the bill will come up for vote the week after. Then I think you can let the press know of your great discovery," Jackson said. He took out a blank piece of paper with no header. He wrote the name of the contact for construction and the amount needed. He folded the paper and handed it to John.

John opened it and sighed, as it was a reasonable six-figure amount. "Not a problem. I'm glad to help," he said and smiled.

Jackson stood up and stuck out his hand. "John, it was a pleasure to meet you. I was happy to be able to help you. I wish you the best of luck with all your future endeavors."

"Thank you, Congressman. It was a real pleasure. The whole company will be ecstatic. You have helped open a new chapter at Quality Seed. Again, many thanks." John shook his hand vigorously.

"Good, good. Safe travels back to Indiana," Jackson said.

John left the office and smiled all the way to Indiana.

Chapter 19

"Hey, Jorge, we did it," John said enthusiastically in his Quality Seed headquarters office. He moved his swivel chair back and forth.

"You did what, little brother?" Jorge's voice on his cell phone was difficult to hear with the wind blowing past his microphone. He was on the dock in Savannah gathering some items for a boat trip.

"The press from *Agriculture Technology and Finance Magazine* will be coming to my office in the next hour or so, and we are officially releasing the MDMV-enhanced corn. We actually have been preparing for the last two months and have delivered MDMV and the solution to some commercial farms in anticipation of the release. The bill exempting MDMV-enhanced corn from GMO labeling finally was signed by the president, and we are ready for release to the general public," John said, stammering ecstatically.

"Oh, that virus thing. So you think that is going to work out?" Jorge asked in a somewhat disinterested way.

"It's going to more than work out. Are you in the middle of something? You sound as if you are distracted," John asked, a bit annoyed that Jorge was not rejoicing as much as he was.

"I'm packing some gear to go camping on a tiny island off the coast. I sold some art during the week and thought I would take a break and come up with some more ideas."

"Maybe you are not getting the implications of what I'm telling you. You are going to be a very wealthy man after this announcement. Your shares may quadruple in value. Not only that, it is a new chapter in Quality Seed. For so long, we had been the company tagging along with the other companies. We were trying to fend off buyouts by people like Ingersoll and avert bankruptcy from companies like AgWorld waging price wars with us. We are not just the nice company, the quality company, but we are now *the innovative company.*"

"That's great, John. Congratulations. I am already a wealthy man. Look at the way I live. I'll check that share price of mine when I get back in a week or so. But one thing: They let the MDMV sail through Congress without further safety studies?" Jorge asked. Jorge, with his distant biology background had thought, since his brother's visit, that long safety trials with the newly enhanced corn would have drained Quality Seed's research-and-development fund and thus prevented long-term success of the company. He never expressed these ideas to John, as he did not want to blunt his brother's enthusiasm.

"Turns out Vivek Satchinanda helped me before he left. He called NOGMO to look at the MDMV corn, and they ended up endorsing us," John said.

"Satchinanda left? Hmm. That's too bad," Jorge said. Despite never meeting the scientist, Jorge had heard from his brother that Dr. Satchinanda looked after the company as if it were his own. Jorge thought it was odd but didn't feel it was necessary to interrogate John about this further, as he really only knew the man peripherally, and there could be infinite reasons why he left.

"Yeah. Too bad. But we are still doing great," John said in a positive tone.

"So did you tell Dad the good news?" Jorge asked.

"No, I want to do it tomorrow. The article will come out later today. Then, after the opening of stock market tomorrow, we can see the share price climbing. I'll call him in the afternoon. Maybe they will get me to do the closing gavel by the end of the week."

"I look forward to seeing that. Well, good luck today and tomorrow. Give a kiss to your missus and my niece and nephew for me."

"Thanks. Will do. I greatly appreciate your confidence in me, bro," John said.

"No prob," Jorge said and hung up the phone. He started the engine of his boat and headed to his desolate-island camping spot.

John put his phone in his pocket and stood up to put on his navy-blue suit jacket. He pulled this over his white shirt and buttoned it on top of a bright-red power tie. Sitting back in his chair, he looked over some notes before the reporter arrived.

A very young-looking, thin Asian man came into John's office, carrying a mini–digital camera attached to a tripod, and slung over his shoulder was a leather satchel. He wore black glasses and had spiky, gel-encrusted hair. He wore a brown blazer and a tan shirt and plaid pants, which made him look as if he came straight off the pages of a men's fashion magazine. "Hi, Mr. Mend. Quinton Kim. Nice to meet you." He stuck out his hand.

"Hi, nice to meet you. John, please. A camera?" John asked and shook his hand.

"Yes. I hope you don't mind. I will record this and then go back to my office to finish my article about you and Quality Seed's new product. I'm planning on having the online article out by this afternoon, and we'll be in print by tomorrow," Quinton said, and began to set up his tripod.

"No camera crew?" John said, to lighten the mood.

"Our media doesn't make as much money as it used to. We need to save as much as we can," Quinton said and screwed the camera onto the tripod. "Let's start rolling, OK?"

"Sure. Where do you want to begin?"

Quinton went into his leather satchel and pulled out a tablet computer. He had a list of his questions on the screen. "Well, let's start out with the new product you have. What is it, and what can we expect from it?

"It is technically called Quality Seed MDMV-enhanced corn. It has exceptional flavor, grows in a short amount of time, and produces yields twenty percent greater than what is on the current market. Let me show you a presentation on my computer. I'm not sure it will show up on your camera," John said.

"No worries. We have done this before. Go ahead," Quinton said.

John turned the flat-screen of his desktop computer toward Quinton and the camera. Over the next forty-five minutes, he went over the mechanics of the MDMV corn, the taste tests that were performed, the yield data that he had, and finally the projected sales and profits to Quality Seed.

"Oh wow, that is great. Are there any safety concerns?" Quinton asked, the end of his pen on his bottom lip.

"We have been vetted by no other than the great nonpartisan scientists affiliated with NOGMO," John said confidently.

"That will be a relief to many folks. It sounds as if you have a completely new way of doing things that is good for the population and good for your bottom line," Quinton said.

"Absolutely."

"So where is it being distributed?"

"We are our own distributer of the preparation chemicals and MDMV solution. This has gone to several commercial and commercial-affiliated farmers. As I understand it from our commercial-farmer purchasing partners, you will see the corn on store shelves very soon. It will initially be unprocessed and sold in The General Store locations and the Human Granary grocery stores all across the country," John said.

"It's great news for Quality Seed that big retailers are carrying this. I look forward to eating some of the Quality Seed MDMV-enhanced corn next week. John, thank you for your time." Quinton stood up and stuck out his hand.

"Anytime. Thank you for the exposure. Do you need any help?" John asked.

Quinton shook his head, tossed his tablet computer into his satchel, folded his tripod, and quickly walked out the door.

The next morning, the story was all over the news. The release of the corn received a lot of fanfare. One paper's headline said, "QUALITY SEED CREATES GAME CHANGER IN CORN PRODUCTION." John had decided to stay in his home office and field questions from various news organizations. While he was fielding calls, he looked at share prices and saw them climb steadily with almost no plateau.

After a break in the action, he decided to call his father. "Hi, Dad, how are you doing?"

On the other end, his father said, "John, you are quite the independent man."

John was puzzled. His father had always called him by his birth name, Juan, and not John, which John had insisted his father do. But at this moment, when he wanted recognition from his father, he felt a pang in his stomach, yearning for a connection to his heritage. For the first time since he was a boy, he wanted his father to call him Juan. In the end, he gave his father all the credit for his success. "Dad, if it weren't for you, there would be no Quality Seed. At this moment, I feel as if the reason I have wanted to achieve greatness completely on my own was in a way to please you."

"You didn't need to do that. I have always been proud of you," his father said.

"Thanks, Dad. When do you want to come and celebrate?" John asked with jubilation.

"Tell me when."

"Definitely. Ah, Dad, a call from another news organization is coming through."

"Enjoy the moment. Hug my grandchildren for me," his father said.

"OK, Dad, love you. Good-bye." John quickly hung up the phone.

He picked up the other line and looked with great appreciation at an article from the 1950s, featuring his father as the innovator at the new Quality Seed Company.

By midafternoon, his interviews were finished, and he left his headquarters office for his home office. The bell rang at the Mend residence, and John answered the door. A delivery man in a brown uniform was holding a wooden bucket full of Quality Seed MDMV-enhanced corn. A few of the husks were opened, and the yellow kernels inside seemed to glisten in the sunlight.

"Honey, it's here. We are going to eat well tonight," John said in a loud, excited voice to his wife, Jaqueline, who was in the kitchen. "Please bring it in here," he said and motioned to the delivery man to bring it into the kitchen.

His wife was in the kitchen snacking on some carrots. She smiled at the delivery man. "Well, I guess I know what we are having for dinner," she said to John.

The delivery man deposited the basket of corn on a dark-marble kitchen island and walked out of the house.

"It's here. The final product. This right here is what will make generations of the Mend family set for life." He pointed to the basket and gave his wife a hug and kiss.

His very thin wife smiled widely and pressed her nose to his. She hadn't seen John this excited in years. "Margarita," she yelled upstairs. "It appears Mr. Mend has given us a project."

Margarita Sanchez came downstairs. The three of them worked hard to prepare an extravagant meal to celebrate Quality Seed's success. Margarita went home before their meal. The whole Mend family sat around a large, round mahogany table. John said a prayer of thanks with Jaqueline, Valencia, his oldest child, and Michael, his youngest, at the table. He was looking forward to tasting his success. He had last eaten an ear of this corn about a week ago and was very impressed by the results. The family gorged themselves as if it were Thanksgiving, with prime rib as the entrée instead of turkey. The delicious corn was not only in cob form but was in all the side dishes, too: a salad, cornbread, and salsa.

After dinner, John went downstairs to his office, as he had numerous messages. One call he received was from Vivek Satchinanda. He called him back.

"Vivek, I'm sorry I missed your call," John said sincerely.

"I just wanted to say congratulations and best wishes," Vivek said.

"Thank you. You know you can come back anytime."

"Thank you but—"

"Hang on, Vivek."

Jacqueline had just stepped into the office to give her husband a glass of wine. John grabbed the glass and smiled at her in thanks.

"Ahhh! Mommy, my stomach is hurting me!" Michael's voice screeched from upstairs.

John covered up the phone. "Jackie, can you see what is bothering him? I'm on the phone with Vivek. He probably just ate too much."

Jaqueline left her glass of wine on his desk and ran upstairs to address Michael.

"Everything OK, John?" Vivek asked.

"Yes, fine. We just had a fabulous dinner with the new corn," John explained. He wiped his brow with his sleeve, as he was feeling very warm suddenly.

"I wish I could stay, but you have other priorities with regard to the direction for the company…"

John zoned out from Vivek's talking and felt a droplet coming down from his nose. He wiped his nose with the back of his sleeve. The white sleeve had a bright-red blotch on it.

"I hope we can remain friends," Vivek said.

"John, come quick! I need you!" Jaqueline's scream from upstairs cut into the air.

"Sure, yeah, no problem." John, distracted by Jacqueline's scream and the blood on his sleeve, hung the phone up quickly and put it in his pocket.

John ran up the spiral staircase. He heard loud music coming from Valencia's room. He turned quickly into Michael's room. Bloody vomit was all over the side table and rug. Michael was face down on his bed, not moving.

"Oh my God! Jackie, what happened!" John gasped at the scene in absolute terror.

"Michael isn't breathing," Jackie said, barely audible, gasping for air. She looked pale. She was taking deep breaths. Blood was on her blouse. Blood was also coming from her nose and ears.

John was confused about what to do. He was feeling scorching hot, but in an instant ignored this feeling and ran toward Michael. He shook the pale, lifeless boy. "Michael, wake up!" He didn't know CPR but remembered seeing how on TV actors would listen for breaths and feel a pulse. He felt nothing.

John then noticed that Jacqueline had stopped breathing. She had kneeled midway down Michael's bed in prayer. He called out to her as well.

"Jacqueline! Wake up!" She didn't respond. He then felt the worst headache of his life.

He pulled out his phone and flipped through the screens to get to his dialing pad. As soon as he did, everything went blurry and red colored. He couldn't see the numbers on his phone to dial 911. He called out to his daughter, "Valencia! Valencia! Help me!" He used his arms to guide him through Michael's doorway and started down the hall to her room. "Valencia!" he called out one last time and fell to the floor in the middle of the hallway, with his arms spread out.

About thirty minutes later, Valencia, who was in her own little world, listening to music, came out of her room. She saw her father lying in his own blood in the hallway and then saw her mother and brother lying bloody in bed, and she cried out for all of them. In a panic, she ran out of the house and into the cabana by the pool in the backyard.

Chapter 20

"So what's the good word, Doc?" Officer Sammy Grillo rubbed his eyes as he asked the question. He had been in a small waiting room, dozing off during the night. Sammy was concerned that the Mend family had been poisoned and was standing guard in case whoever did this wanted to finish the job. George, seated next to him, was still sleeping.

"There's no need to transfer her to a new hospital," Dr. Harper said. He had a very grim expression on his face. Black circles below his eyes were still very visible despite his brown complexion.

"What? Why not?" Sammy said, all excited.

"She died last night, about four or five hours ago. I didn't want to wake you," Dr. Harper said grimly.

"What caused this? Do you think it was poison?"

"Essentially, she bled to death. We have sent out toxicology specimens. I had one of the pathologists, though, look at a small skin biopsy of a bleeding lesion and give me a preliminary report. He says it looks like a hemorrhagic-type fever that is typically seen by a virus."

"How did she get that?"

"I'm not exactly sure of the route of entry of the virus. But if what you told me about the rest of the family is true, then it must be something everyone caught. She had told me in a few delirious moments that the family had just celebrated their father's new corn product. I had read about it in one of the financial rags this morning. Corn would be a very odd way for a virus to get into the body, but I'm sure it is possible. I have contacted the state infection bureau and alerted the Centers for Disease Control and Prevention as well. They want us to take some precautions until they can find out more."

"What kind of precautions?"

"I think anyone who has had contact with this girl needs to be quarantined. That means you two should stay here for a few days, as well as anyone else from your team. The EMTs and the housekeeper also should come here," Dr. Harper said and pushed his metal-framed glasses up his nose.

"How long do we need to stay?"

"It looks like, if it is a virus, it infects people very rapidly. I suspect a couple of days, but by then the CDC will be here to give us more information."

"OK, I guess we're stuck here," Sammy said, and nudged George, who had his arms crossed and was snoring. "Wake up!"

"Huh? Wha? What's going on?" George asked.

"Unfortunately, the girl, Valencia, died last night. Doc, here, thinks it's infectious, and he wants anyone in contact to stay here a few days so we don't pass this to anyone else if we have it," Sammy said.

"So we may have this?" George was alarmed.

Dr. Harper chimed in. "It is unlikely that you all have the virus, as this affected the family so quickly, and I would think you two would be showing some signs and symptoms of infection. But we should take precautions just in case we need to address your symptoms right away and prevent you from passing this to anyone else you may meet."

George nodded and stretched his legs. "I'll call Joe and ask him to bring Lenny here."

"George, we also need Miss Sanchez and the EMTs who assisted us last night to come here as well," Sammy said.

"OK, boss, I'll get on it," George said. He pressed the button on his radio to get in touch with Joe. "Hey, Joe, we need you to get Lenny and possibly Miss Sanchez over to the hospital right away. Sounds like this is an infection, and we need to be quarantined for a few days."

He heard nothing over the radio. "Joe, you there? Answer me. Should have clocked in by now."

"Yeah, George. I'm on my way there right now. I have Lenny here, and he's looking pretty bad. He looks a lot like the family in the house. He is barely awake. He's got blood running down his nose. I picked him up from his house, and then he just passed out in my car!" Joe's voice was clipped and panicky.

"Hurry up. We will be waiting for you. I'll tell Dr. Harper," George said.

"Boss, Lenny has gotten sick," George said to Sammy and Dr. Harper, who were in the middle of discussing the process for quarantine.

"Give me your radio. I have to call dispatch," Sammy said and took his radio. He called dispatch to have a car sent for Miss Sanchez and to send in the EMTs from yesterday's call.

"I hope for all of our sakes that this disease stays contained," Dr. Harper said in a deflated tone, knowing very well that that was unlikely to be the case.

⚕

It was a warm summer day in Chicago. The sky was partly cloudy, allowing for some relief from the summer sun. Eric Feldberg sat at a glass table on the deck of his penthouse suite. He was looking at his tablet computer. Earbuds shut out the world around him. A podcast of the latest news was on his computer.

The news was clogged with stories about the recent hemorrhagic-fever epidemic.

We have heard that about one thousand people from coast to coast have died, and thousands more are infected in the short course of a week. The source of the infection appears to be corn that was enhanced by a specially designed maize dwarf mosaic virus. According to scientists from the Centers for Disease Control and Prevention, this virus that usually infects corn now is infecting people. The symptoms of infection include a sudden onset of fever and bleeding of the nose, ears, mouth, eyes, and rectum. The CDC advises anyone with these symptoms to call nine-one-one. State officials have set up special teams to retrieve people infected with the virus. Communities that have been affected and even state officials have begun to call the instigator of this illness "the Red Corn," due to the bloody fever and not the actual color of the corn. The best way to prevent infection is to avoid eating or having any type of contact with the Red Corn which comes from Quality Seed. Signs in towns around the country say, "Do not eat the red corn."

Eric took the earbuds out of his ears and stood up. He wanted to stretch his legs a little. He leaned his elbows on the railing of the courtyard and looked out. Then he focused back on his tablet at the recent stock prices. The price of Quality Seed stock sunk like a stone and had been falling like this since the death of John Mend. Shareholders sensed a lack of leadership at the company, causing an early downturn in stock price, which plateaued for a day. The news trickled out that Quality Seed's product was killing hundreds, if not thousands, of people, and the shares tanked. Eric was somewhat miffed that John didn't get to see Quality Seed fall apart. Eric liked to see adversaries completely vanquished. Quality Seed was predicted to file for bankruptcy in order to protect itself from the many lawsuits looming ahead. Eric looked out at the skyscrapers again and smiled at his accomplishments.

A beeping sound came from the table. It was Marco Brunelli, AgWorld's chief financial officer. AgWorld's stock was also taking a hit with the hemorrhagic fever, because if too many people died, there would be no one to purchase goods and services. Eric was hoping Marco was not panicking. "Yep, what is it?" Eric answered as if he was being pestered.

"You see what Quality Seed stock is doing?" Marco asked excitedly.

"Yes, and I think that is a good thing," Eric said calmly.

"I have Roger Ingersoll on the other line, and he would like to get rid of some of Quality Seed's assets before the complete implosion of the company."

Eric disliked fund managers like Ingersoll. Fund managers always seemed to ruin a company's best-laid plans. Eric was able to play each fund manager off each other to prevent them from meddling in AgWorld's affairs. "Let Mr.

Ingersoll know that if he really needs cash, a great little corner a few blocks from my place has great panhandling," he told Marco.

"You're joking," Marco said, aghast.

"No, I don't want any of his infected assets. Just relay it to him exactly the way I told you."

"OK," Marco said nervously. He was hoping for some clarification from Eric.

"Good-bye." Eric hung up. He felt like an exterminator who had gotten rid of so many pests.

Melissa, his wife, was dressed in heels, short skirt, and a blouse, looking as if she was heading out on the town as she came out to the porch, carrying their baby. Annabelle was cooing under a blanket.

"Have you heard the news?" she asked, bouncing the baby up and down.

"Yes, Quality Seed is history," Eric said and smiled.

"What? No, there is a plague, and people are dying!" Melissa said in a panic, not understanding why Eric was so gleeful about a company's demise during what she thought might be the end of the world.

"I did hear something about that," Eric said casually.

"Shouldn't we get out of the city? It seems as if it would be a lot easier getting that disease where there are a lot of people."

"Possibly."

"Well, I was planning on taking Annabelle with me to my aunt's cabin outside of Madison. I tried calling Ayanna to see if she would want to come and help out. She didn't answer. I almost think she may be ill as well." Melissa was desperate for a protective response from Eric.

"Sounds like a plan," Eric said flatly and looked at his tablet computer.

"Well, I guess I'll get going. Do you know how to get to her house?" Melissa asked.

"I think I remember," he mumbled into his tablet, as if he was not concerned about reaching the "safe zone."

"Good-bye," Melissa said, and she paused at the door to the patio, waiting for acknowledgment that never came. She wished, at the precipice of the end of the world, that she could get from the man she married an "I love you."

"Safe travels," Eric said into his computer.

Melissa stomped off angry and sad. She grabbed a duffel bag and a purse and slammed the door behind her.

Once Eric heard the door close, he put aside his computer, put his legs on the table, and clasped his hands behind his head. At that moment, he thought he would sunbathe in paradise on this perfect day.

⚔

Daisy put her groceries down on the kitchen counter. She was excited to be seeing Jessica again. Apparently getting the funding for NOGMO from Eric made for even more work and travel for the agency. Jessica had told her a few days ago when she left that she didn't need to come on this trip. Daisy thought things had been getting better with Jessica. Maybe now that the financial stress of NOGMO and keeping the house was behind them, she could work on her relationship even more. The "red-corn" scare had just started, and she was scared that Jessica might have gotten infected. The large grocery store that she frequented and that claimed to sell only nonmodified food had pulled all of its corn on the cob, frozen corn, and even processed corn products just in case. She had bought some free-range chicken, as well as broccoli, cauliflower, carrots, and peas. The plan was to make Jessica's favorite stir-fry.

Daisy lit a spiced candle before starting to chop her ingredients. By the candle she noticed a little folded note and opened it. It was a letter written in Jessica's beautiful cursive, dated that day.

Daisy,

I am writing this letter to let you know how much you betrayed me and NOGMO. I did not want to do this in person, to avoid a shouting match or even violence toward you. I have evidence that you slept with, of all people, Eric Feldberg of AgWorld. That man is completely anathema to the mission of NOGMO. Not to mention, you compromised our relationship. The last few years I have been carrying your weight at NOGMO, but still I told everyone that we were partners there. I had thought we had a real relationship, but apparently you may have needed a security blanket to toss around whenever you got your confidence going. I have evidence to suggest he has been texting you and has continued to do so up until even six weeks ago. Once I heard the interview with John Mend that suggested we endorsed his corn, I knew I couldn't trust you or possibly get an honest answer out of you. I suspect the sudden influx of cash to us and NOGMO had something to do with the endorsement. Now look at what has happened, and it is partly our fault for endorsing the "red corn."

As of today, I have resigned as the head of NOGMO and have told the office to assign you as the interim head of the organization. I suspect there may be reporters and the FDA asking what made NOGMO endorse such a lethally modified food. You got NOGMO into this mess, and if it is to remain an entity, you can get it out of this, maybe even with a little help from your boyfriend. I will be writing an editorial for a national paper absolving myself from this mess. As for me and what was us, I have found an attorney who will separate the assets, including the house. You can keep any money from your boyfriend. I want nothing to do with it. I will have a friend help move my belongings.

Life takes people on many twists and turns, and I was really hoping you and I could straighten them out together. Don't bother trying to apologize or contacting me. At this point, I don't see me ever speaking to you again.
Jessica

As Daisy read, tears came down her face and hit Jessica's note. She brought the paper to her nose and wailed. All her guilt and sadness came pouring out, and a deep loneliness enveloped her. After a few moments, she stopped crying and grabbed her phone. She pushed **1** to speed-dial Jessica. She was going to apologize and ask her to take her back with whatever conditions she demanded. She was going to tell her that Eric was a mistake and that the only reason she communicated with him was to keep them together and to help NOGMO through their financial issues.

"The number you have dialed is no longer in service. Please check the number—"

Daisy hung up the phone, and her body went limp. Her phone started to ring, and she straightened up and with hope looked to see who it was.

Her caller ID said, "Food and Drug Administration."

⅄

Jorge Mendosa climbed out of his boat and started to unload his gear. The week away was very relaxing. Jorge was always stressed by the littlest of things, and it kept him from working at Quality Seed. Time away from people and immersed in the peacefulness of nature made him feel whole. Jorge scratched the stubbly beard that had grown while he was camping and looked toward the end of the dock, where a young man was waving to him.

"Come quick, Jorge. You are a celebrity," the young man said, with a slurred tongue.

"Hey, Timothy, nice to see you. Where is your uncle Jeff?" Jorge asked and patted the young man on the back. He didn't quite understand why Timothy was out there by himself. Timothy had anoxic brain injury from birth and had a low IQ and a slight limp. His uncle Jeff let him work there to keep him busy, but Jeff was scared to let him out on the docks alone, as he thought Timothy would fall in the water and drown.

"I don't think he's feeling too good. I think he ate the red corn. But come see in the parking lot. A lot of people are waiting for you," Timothy said eagerly.

Jorge was even more puzzled about Timothy's "red corn" comment. When Jorge was out camping, he was completely isolated, and his phone did not get a signal, so he did not know about the recent plague. He humored him and said, "OK, OK, Timothy. Let's see the party."

The two walked toward the parking lot. Numerous vans were parked in a hodgepodge fashion, not obeying any of the lines on the asphalt. The vans had large antennae mounted on them and had different numbers with various call letters indicating the TV stations. Men and women dressed very well with microphones in front of their faces were lined up in the parking lot. Behind the cameras he saw men wearing T-shirts and loose pants with multiple pockets.

Timothy had a broad smile on his face, as if he believed he was standing next to a celebrity.

One of the men, in a brown suit, came up to him. "Mr. Mendosa, did you know that your brother was going to release a deadly virus on humanity?" he asked.

The other reporters also made their way toward him with their microphones pointed toward Jorge's face.

Jorge was taken aback. He had thought the reporters were there to congratulate him on the new product from Quality Seed. He didn't understand the question at all. "I don't know what you mean," he said.

"The red corn. Did you or your brother knowingly poison people with the transformed virus?" a woman in a blue dress asked him.

"What is everyone talking about, this red corn?" he said in a loud voice to the crowd.

A petite reporter in a yellow dress said, "You mean you don't know? The corn transformed by the MDMV virus has unleashed an epidemic of hemorrhagic fever on the country."

"No. I had no idea," Jorge said softly.

"How do you not know? You were his brother. You have the second-highest number of shares. You are a trained biologist. Wouldn't he have run the plan by you?" A reporter in a blue blazer rattled off the questions.

"He ran this by me briefly. His plans sounded fine with me. I didn't go through the nuts and bolts of his plan. I have nothing to do with the day-to-day operations of the company. I have been away for a week. Why aren't you asking my brother?" he said, pleading. This inquisition brought back all the anxiety and stress that he left one week ago.

A male reporter in a gray suit behind the crowd said in a loud voice, "We'd love to, but he's dead."

Jorge's heart began to race, and his head swam. The reporters kept asking questions over each other, and it blended into a horrifying cacophony. He turned to Timothy, who was standing next to him, and handed him some cash. "Get one of the boys to fill the tank, and tell them to hurry."

During the inquisition, Timothy had had a broad smile on his face. "OK, Jorge."

"We are sorry if we are interrupting you, but America wants answers!" the journalist with the blue dress said.

"If you're not going to answer us, then there are a couple of federal agents who want to question you," the journalist in the gray suit said.

Two men who were leaning against a black sedan came off the vehicle and started walking toward the group of journalists.

"I'm sorry. This is a lot to digest, and I was about to unload my boat here. If you all would wait a few minutes while I get myself together, I can talk to you for a good long while." He smiled and backed away from the crowd. He walked toward his boat. A boy from the store's station was filling his tank. He took a bag out of his boat and looked around in it. He could see that the reporters and journalists were observing his rifling. He looked up from his bag and waved to the reporters.

"All full," the freckled boy said to Jorge.

He gave him twenty dollars above the cost of the gas. "Thanks again. Tell those kind folks up there I will be up in a minute," he said to the boy.

Perfectly timed, another boat's engine started.

Jorge put all his bags in his boat and started his engine. He watched as the boy distracted the crowd. He waved to Timothy, who had been watching him and smiling the entire time he loaded the boat. He edged the throttle forward, and the boat lurched ahead and left the dock.

⋏

Many of the managers of Quality Seed deferred to public-relations people when reporters or government agents asked about the MDMV-enhanced corn. They truly did not know much, anyway. John Mend kept the project small to prevent corporate spies from stealing the ideas. Vivek Satchinanda told people what he knew, but he also told them he left due to the lack of safety studies and alerted the proper authorities. The next person in the chain would be Barry Orr. Finally, agents from the Office of Criminal Investigations, who investigate for the FDA, got to Barry's name.

Barry had been flitting between his home and office. He had talked to one reporter about John's death. He didn't make any connections between the corn and his family's demise. Since then, he had followed the stories of the hemorrhagic fever. He was devastated when the CDC tied the fever to the corn he created. The MDMV was a corn virus and wouldn't infect people, and he had gone over and over this in his mind. His studies with different viruses in rice did not seem to cause untoward effects on people, but he never had real safety studies for that product, either. When NOGMO endorsed the product, he felt a bit relieved and vindicated in his beliefs. Now guilt had crept in. He still thought this was a spontaneous mutation in the virus's DNA that he hadn't made. The fever was not directly his fault, as no one knew this virus could have the capability of infecting people.

Guilt was beginning to settle in his mind. He created the monster, and if anything, he wanted it to kill him off. He had been sitting in his lab office with a big bowl of ears of MDMV-enhanced corn. He was feeling fairly stuffed, as he had eaten about five ears. Other than feeling full, he wasn't warm or bleeding. The course of the illness seemed to occur within an hour to a day of ingestion. He was hoping it was not a day, as he wanted this over and done with.

The phone rang in his office. He could barely hear it. In the midst of his ingestion of corn and self-pity, he had been blasting a mix tape that Vivek Satchinanda made for him. The old magnetic tape crackled the Mickey Gilley song, "Don't the Girls All Get Prettier at Closing Time." Barry turned down the boom box and picked up the phone.

"Dr. Orr, some agents are here to see you about the corn," John's secretary said on the line.

"Please let them know that I'll be out to meet them in just a minute. I'm doing a critical experiment, and I can't come right away," Barry said.

"I will, Dr. Orr," she said and hung up the phone.

He wanted out on his own terms. He didn't want to be a legal pincushion sitting on trial for poisoning America. For Barry, innovation had its price, but most times it worked out. This time it didn't, and if he wanted to suffer, it would be by his own hands. He stuffed the remaining ears of corn in his lab coat and walked out the door. He took the back fire stairs to avoid being seen by the investigators.

Barry had known that he was going to be questioned by reporters or the government at some point, so he'd parked his car about five hundred feet from the Quality Seed headquarters in the distant corner of another company's corporate headquarters. Ducking behind bushes, he made it to his car. He jumped inside his 1968 Buick GS convertible and started the engine. The vehicle was not the subtlest of machines, and the exhaust of his car glugged along as he made his way to his house via back roads.

Once he made it to his house, he packed a few bags and left his cell phone in his house to prevent the government from following him. He then drove to the local branch of his bank that he always went to and withdrew in cash the maximum from his account. The authorities, he believed, would be following him electronically through purchases. He decided to head west, as there was more space to blend in.

He drove until dark, stopping only for bathroom breaks and gas fill-ups. In his 1960s car, that was frequent, even when following reasonable speed limits. When he got tired, he parked his car in an Oklahoma state park. He paid cash for a tent campsite. Dumping his lab coat in the fire pit, he ignited it with lighter fluid from the camp store. He threw the remainder of the corn cobs he ate in there as well. When the fire went out, he planned what he would do next. Other than wait for the hemorrhagic fever to take him, he couldn't think of anything else to do if he survived. He fell asleep in his car thinking.

He woke up the next morning, a little surprised that he survived. He knew from his study of viruses that infection had to do with susceptibility and dosage of exposure. The large amount of corn he ate should have been an adequate dosage. He could not predict in himself susceptibility to the virus. People who were susceptible to an infectious agent were immunocompromised at some level. Barry, despite his horrible lifestyle, was in good shape or just genetically in good shape, when it came to this particular virus.

With no direction, he continued west on the highway. He kept driving until he got tired and stopped at a small town in Nevada just east of California. The one little bar in the town happened to be open. Barry walked in. Hardly any people were inside. The bar was Western themed, with old rifles on the wall and at least five steer skulls with large horns adorning different walls. Various alcohol-brand neon signs were arranged above the bar.

"What'll you have?" a heavyset, balding bartender wearing a stained white shirt said in a gruff New York accent.

"Whiskey straight," Barry said curtly and downed his whiskey immediately.

"You stickin' around tonight?" the bartender asked.

"Maybe. Are you looking for a date?" Barry asked jokingly.

"Yeah, right." The bartender giggled. "Just askin'. There aren't a heck of a lot of places to stay around here."

"A place across the street has a vacancy sign."

"That place is a one-night-stand kind of place. As I implied, I ain't interested."

"Well, where do you suggest?"

"I would suggest a place about a mile or two up the road," the bartender said, wiping the counter.

"Why do you care?"

"I figure you might want to tie one on, and you ain't got a designated driver."

"I want to drink. I'll take my chances next door. Give me another whiskey."

The bartender poured him another whiskey.

Barry paid him for both drinks with a generous tip. He watched the big-screen TV, which was showing the news. Underneath the reporter, who was at a hospital, a caption read, "Overnight, double the number of people have died of hemorrhagic fever. Cases are being found that are unrelated to corn ingestion, and it is suggested that transmission may even be person to person."

"Those greedy bastards. Why did they have to mess with nature?" The bartender shook his fist at the television.

"Possibly they wanted to make life a little better," Barry said, staring at his half-empty shot glass.

"Well, they didn't."

"Nope. They didn't," Barry said flatly and put down his now-empty shot glass.

"I hope those bastards die from that virus. Better yet, I hope the carnage eats them up inside so bad that they wish they were dead," the bartender said in a strident voice.

"Yep. I'm sure they will," Barry said barely audibly and pointed his shot glass at the bartender for a refill.